THE SOUND OF HELICOPTER ROTORS TORE THROUGH THE JUNGLE

"Gunships!" Mack Bolan shouted. "Take cover!"

The night was shattered as a searchlight clicked on under one of the Hinds. The gunship roared overhead, then circled back, playing the light over the trees.

When the aircraft passed close to their hiding place, McCarter knew he'd have the perfect shot. He stepped from cover, his RPG-7 launcher balanced on his shoulder. Just as the cone of light struck him, he triggered the weapon. The rocket burst from the tube with a whoosh, trailing flame when the prop charge kicked in.

The rocket slammed into the underside of the ship and detonated, the warhead easily penetrating the armor. Red-hot shrapnel pierced the fuel tanks, and the aircraft disappeared in a massive explosion.

Undaunted, the second Hind bore in on them in a strafing run, firing its rocket pods and machine guns into the dark. The Stony Man warriors had no choice but to retreat deeper into the jungle, pursued relentlessly.

They were nowhere near the beach, and zero hour was fast approaching....

DON PENDLETON'S
MACK BOLAN®
STONY MAN™
WARHEAD

A GOLD EAGLE BOOK FROM
WORLDWIDE®

TORONTO • NEW YORK • LONDON
AMSTERDAM • PARIS • SYDNEY • HAMBURG
STOCKHOLM • ATHENS • TOKYO • MILAN
MADRID • WARSAW • BUDAPEST • AUCKLAND

First edition November 1994

ISBN 0-373-61897-2

Special thanks and acknowledgment to
Michael Kasner for his contribution to this work.

WARHEAD

WARHEAD

CHAPTER ONE

Southwestern Russia

Major Valery Shernikov, Russian army missile artillery, brought his field glasses to his eyes and scanned the dusty road in front of his small convoy. The landscape along the Russian-Kazakhstan border was harsh, a barren track of sunbaked, rugged hills and scattered, stunted scrub brush. Even though it was spring, he couldn't tell from the landscape, or from the unrelenting sun frying his brain inside the tanker's helmet he wore.

This was the same kind of terrain he had seen far too much of during the Afghanistan War. And the people who inhabited this desolation were much the same as the Afghans he had fought, as well, God-mad barbarians with little regard for human life, theirs or anyone else's.

When the Red Army finally pulled out of the quagmire of the Afghanistan War, Shernikov had thought that he had seen the last of this blighted end of the world and its miserable inhabitants. But unfortunately that wasn't to be. After having been

comfortably stationed in European Russia for the
past several years, a capricious fate in the form of a
promotion had sent him back to serve his country in
this endless desolation.

The major removed the field glasses from his
eyes. Even though he couldn't see anything wrong,
he felt uneasy. He had the same itching feeling between his shoulder blades he had always gotten right
before screaming Afghan Mujahedeen guerrillas had
blown an ambush on one of his convoys in the hills
outside of Kabul.

Though Russia wasn't at war with the Islamic
population in the southwestern reaches yet, tension
was quickly building in the region. There was even
a pool in the officers mess as to how long it would
be before they started shooting at their onetime Islamic socialist brothers. As far as he was concerned, these convoys were a drastic mistake, a
purely political decision that the army would have
to pay for, sooner or later, with its blood.

As part of the great stand-down of the once glo-
rious Red Army, the tactical nuclear missiles were
being withdrawn as fast as they could be from the
dismantled Soviet Union. Shernikov's convoy with
its ten nuclear warheads was only one of many such
convoys carrying deadly cargoes back to safety inside the European Russian heartland. None of them
had experienced any problems with the locals so far,

and Shernikov was determined that this convoy would make it to safety, as well.

He would have felt more comfortable if he'd had a full-strength motorized rifle battalion riding with him. He had requested the infantry escort, but that didn't fit in with the Russian president's grand strategy. The man wanted to get the nukes back where he could keep a better eye on them, but he didn't want the locals to know that they were being moved. It would be much easier to control the barren tracks of southwestern Russia if their Islamic neighbors believed that the battered Russian bear still had sharp nuclear teeth and claws.

Therefore, the orders had come down that the missile warheads were to be withdrawn in small convoys like his and with only minimum escort. That way, they would look like routine supply convoys to the missile sites rather than a withdrawal of the nuclear weapons.

It all sounded good on paper, but Shernikov wasn't buying any of it. Even though the withdrawal operation had gone smoothly so far, he wasn't about to relax his guard. As far as he was concerned, the longer this operation lasted, the more chance there was that word of it would leak out and some Arab leader would get the bright idea to try to grab a nuke or two for his own use. He didn't even want to think of what would happen if that occurred.

Looking back and seeing that the convoy's trail vehicle was lagging behind, Shernikov keyed his throat mike.

"Bird Dog, this is Fox Hound," he called back to Lieutenant Yuri Vanavitch, his assistant convoy control officer. "For the last time, Yuri, close it up and watch your intervals. This is supposed to be a tight supply convoy, not a tactical formation."

"Closing up now," Vanavitch replied.

The lieutenant was a good man, but he had been reading too many Afghan War novels lately. In this situation, their best defense was to keep it tight.

A few minutes later, when the major heard the sound of approaching helicopters, he frowned. He had also requested a gunship escort, but like the request for the motorized rifle battalion, it too had been turned down. Maybe the commander of the military district had decided that it wouldn't hurt to have some aerial firepower on hand.

Bringing up his field glasses, he saw that the approaching choppers had the familiar silhouettes of late-model Russian Mi-24 gunships. Nicknamed Gorbach, the Hunchback, by the Red Army, the Americans had code-named the flying battleships the Hind. He didn't understand how the world's largest assault helicopter could be named after a small deer, but no one could understand those crazy Yankees anyway.

When one of the gunships broke away from the flight and flew parallel to the convoy, Shernikov noticed that it was painted in fresh Afghan-style earth-and-sand-colored camouflage. Bringing his field glasses up again, he saw that the machine wasn't bearing the red star markings of the Russian air force. In fact, it had no national insignia of any kind.

That was odd, he thought. But, with the way things were in the fragmented army nowadays, more than likely the ship had just come out of a mainte-nance-facility paint shop and they had been out of stock of the red paint needed to put the markings back on. It had been lucky to have even received proper maintenance, so the lack of national markings could be excused.

Like many officers of the once powerful Red Army, Shernikov wasn't fond of the new civilian-controlled Russian state. The vaunted personal freedoms were welcomed, but they had come with a heavy cost, one that he wasn't sure Russia could afford to pay. As far as he was concerned, the heaviest cost of all had been borne by the armed forces. Recruiting and discipline had gone to hell, but the financial crisis was even worse. The army couldn't even afford adequate training ammunition anymore for the few recruits they did get. If they had to go to war again, even with Arabs, they would be in serious trouble.

Turning in the command hatch of his BDR-70, he followed the lone gunship as it went into a high orbit alongside the dusty road. With his back turned, he didn't see the other three choppers begin their gun run on the rear of his small convoy.

The detonation of the first AT-6 Spiral antitank missile came like a thunderclap. The six-foot missile had homed in on Lieutenant Vanavitch's armored vehicle and had impacted on the top of the engine deck. The explosion of its shaped-charge warhead set off the fuel tanks and turned the vehicle into a blazing inferno.

The first missile was instantly followed by others as the Mi-24s targeted the small convoy. A shattering explosion rocked Shernikov's vehicle, lifting it off of its wheels. When it slammed back down, he was thrown halfway out of the hatch and into the gout of flame that burst from the engine compartment.

The Russian frantically beat at the fire licking at his face and hands. Only the sand goggles saved his eyes. When the flames were extinguished, he painfully crawled the rest of the way out of the command hatch and fell to the ground.

Remembering the way the Mujis had always cleared an ambush zone, shooting everybody, alive or dead, he started scrambling for cover under the side of the command vehicle. He was only halfway under when he heard the choppers land, and he froze where he was, his legs still exposed. If he played dead, he might survive this. It was a big "maybe," but it was the only chance he had. If he tried to run, he'd be gunned down before he made ten meters.

Shouts of triumph in Arabic, cries for mercy in Russian and single shots rang out as the Mujis cleared the ambush site. The shots were coming closer to him.

Forcing himself to keep his eyes open and un-blinking behind his goggles, he saw a face come into his peripheral vision, an Asian face. The man was wearing the same desert camouflage uniform and tan turban as the rest of his men, but Shernikov knew that he wasn't a local. He had gone to service schools in the old Soviet Union with officers of the Asian Communist nations, and this guy was either Chinese or North Korean.

The men with him, however, were Mujahedeen of some variety or the other, Islamic holy warriors. The breeze brought him the smell of rancid sheep fat mixed with wood smoke that was the distinctive odor of the Dushmen.

One of the bandits walked up to him, a gap-toothed, unwashed barbarian with a Russian-made AK-47 assault rifle in his hand. Smiling when he saw the blood and burns on Shernikov's face and his open staring eyes, he casually aimed the assault rifle at his belly and pulled the trigger. The Muji jerked his hand when he fired, and the 7.62 mm bullet hit Shernikov low in the side, tearing a bloody furrow along his lowest rib.

By sheer willpower, the Russian didn't even blink when the round hit him. As he had known it would do, the wound instantly went numb. It wouldn't start to hurt for half an hour or so, and by that time they might be gone. The Muji smiled again and walked out of his line of sight.

Only after putting a bullet in each of the Russians, dead or alive, did the Dushmen approach the two undamaged cargo trucks carrying the ten nuclear warheads.

While some of the Mujis stripped the bodies of weapons and anything they could use, the others quickly took the warheads from the truck beds and carefully loaded them onto the helicopters. The warheads weren't heavy, only about fifty kilos, but two men carried each of the crates as carefully as if they were full of fresh eggs.

As soon as the last warhead had been loaded, a shouted command sent the Mujis running for the choppers. One by one, they lifted off and, keeping low to the ground, flew away to the east.

WHEN THE BEAT of the rotors faded in the distance, Shernikov painfully dragged himself out from under the wrecked command car. A pall of greasy black smoke rose into the clear blue sky from the burning hulks of the other vehicles. The choking smell of burning rubber and oil mixed with the sharp scent of cordite and the bitter, metallic odor of fresh blood. Ammunition cooked off in the fires, adding to the smoke.

Shernikov didn't even bother to check to see if any of his men were alive as he painfully limped over to the first of the now empty cargo trucks. He knew better. It had been a fluke that he had survived. None of the rest of his men would have known enough about the Mujis to play dead.

The first thing he had to do was to see if one of the vehicle first-aid kits had been left behind. Then, once he had bandaged his wound, he needed to find water. The military district commander would send someone to investigate when he didn't make his next scheduled comm check. But, knowing Colonel Denkavitch as he did, Shernikov knew that he would have to call the military region headquarters first and get the general's permission before he moved his troops a meter out of his fortified compound.

Finding a full canteen, he crawled painfully into the back of one of the empty trucks and made himself comfortable. It might be quite some time before he was rescued.

CHAPTER TWO

Stony Man Farm, Virginia

Aaron Kurtzman sat in his wheelchair in front of the picture window in the den of the Stony Man farmhouse and stared out at the dark majesty of the Blue Ridge Mountains. Spring was always a nice time of year in Virginia's Shenandoah Valley. During the Civil War, this had been the "valley of humiliation" for the Union forces as Confederate General Stonewall Jackson had waged his campaigns against the Boys in Blue. Now, it was a national park only eighty miles from Washington, D.C.

Named after Stony Man Mountain, one of the highest peaks in the area, the small farm didn't look much different from the other small farms in the area. In the center of the grounds was a three-story farmhouse, flanked by two outbuildings, with a tractor barn in the back. On the surface, it looked legitimate, complete with farmhands in blue jeans and boots and the well-used machinery necessary for making a living from the earth. The land close to the house was planted in row crops, while apple and peach orchards formed a wall around the perimeter.

The crops were harvested when they were ready for market, and the fruit was picked when it was ripe. But Stony Man Farm was more than just another Shenandoah Valley operation. It was the command center for America's most covert arm of the government, the Justice Department's Sensitive Operations Group. The buildings of the farm concealed the equipment and personnel needed to back up the antiterrorist and antiorganized-crime units that waged war on the nation's most elusive enemies.

Aaron Kurtzman hadn't always been confined to a wheelchair. He was a big man, built like an old-time blacksmith and known as "The Bear" to his intimates. A bullet in the spine had put him in the chair, but it hadn't ended his career as chief intelligence gatherer at the Farm.

The door to the den opened soundlessly and a woman walked into the wood-paneled office, stopping a few feet inside the room. Barbara Price looked like a model, tall, blond and slender, with the high cheek bones that fashion cameras loved. In her tight blue jeans, cowboy boots and chambray shirt, she looked nothing like the mission controller for a top-secret military strike force.

"Aaron," she said, "Jack's chopper is inbound, ETA in ten minutes." "Jack" was Jack Grimaldi, Stony Man's ace fly-boy.

Kurtzman's powerful arms and shoulders spun the chair to face her. "Hal still hasn't told us what's going down?"

She shook her head. "All he's said is that our visitor will brief us and that we are to give him our fullest cooperation."

"But who is this guy?"

"He's some Russian intelligence expert on the Far East, a Lieutenant-Colonel Gregori Klimov."

"Damn," the computer wizard said, clicking the name through the files in his mind. "Klimov is—was—hard-core KGB. He's the bastard who was responsible for the interrogation of American POWs during the Vietnam War, the ones who are still missing."

"You're kidding!"

"No way. Gregori K. Klimov, right?"

Price nodded.

"He was identified last month when the Russians finally turned over that batch of documents regarding the missing POWs they interrogated during the war."

"Wait a sec," Price said, "and let me double-check this guy." She was on the secure phone line to Hal Brognola in Washington a moment later.

On paper, Brognola was a high-ranking agent in the Justice Department and a liaison officer to the Oval Office. In addition to those duties, however, he was the director of the Sensitive Operations Group, the man the President called when lives and the world community were in jeopardy.

Price hung up the handset. "Hal says that the Man has pledged his fullest cooperation on this one."

She took a deep breath. "He also says that this mission has the highest possible priority, and we don't have to like it."

"Okay, okay. Tell Jack to bring the bastard on in."

FOUR ARMED SECURITY MEN dressed like farmhands met Jack Grimaldi's chopper when it landed at the Farm's airstrip, then escorted the unwelcome and blindfolded visitor into the van for the short ride to the farmhouse. Once there, the ex-KGB officer was helped from the vehicle, then subjected to a thorough pat-down for hardware before the door opened to let him in.

The cortege proceeded to the basement level and to a waiting Barbara Price, who admitted the Russian to the War Room. She then removed the blindfold and stepped to one side.

"Aaron Kurtzman—"

The Russian ignored her attempt at introductions and took over.

"Gregori Klimov," he said, bowing slightly from the waist and extending his hand.

Kurtzman ignored the Russian's hand. "You're here against my strongest protests, Klimov. I know who you are. If I had anything to say about it, you'd be dead now. But I've been ordered to work with you, and I will."

Klimov didn't change expression as he withdrew his hand. Even though the Americans had won the cold war, he had met several of them recently who weren't willing to be gracious victors, particularly not to ex-officers of the old, hated Soviet KGB. The organization was dead, and as far as he was concerned, everything he had done as a KGB officer was history, too. And that included his interrogation of American POWs during the Vietnam War.

The business with the POWs had been an operational matter back then, not personal. He wasn't one of those who enjoyed watching another man's suffering, but it had been part of the job. He had always taken his work seriously. If nothing else, Klimov was pragmatic as only a Russian could be. This was a new era, and new times called for new ways of doing things—even if it meant trying to make friends with people who wanted nothing less than his blood. The mission required it.

Sensing that the ball was in his court, Klimov skipped the rest of the introductions and got to the point of his visit. "The situation that has both of our presidents so concerned is that ten tactical nuclear missile warheads have disappeared from a Russian army convoy on the Kazakhstan border."

"That's incredible," Kurtzman replied. "Just how the hell did you manage to do that?"

The Russian ignored Kurtzman's provocative manner. "That's what I came here to tell you," he said patiently.

"You could have written a letter."

"It seems that our presidents felt that it would be best if I delivered this particular message in person."

"Okay, give."

Klimov quickly recounted the circumstances of the aerial ambush of the convoy. "These are not large warheads," he concluded. "As far as nuclear warheads go, only two kiloton yield. Or, a tenth as powerful as the weapon dropped on Hiroshima."

"How do you know the details about the attack?" Price asked. "Specifically that it was lead by a Chinese or Korean officer."

"The convoy commander was wounded, and he survived the attack by playing dead. He made the tentative identification of the hijacker's leader."

"That's convenient."

Klimov ignored Kurtzman's remark and continued. "In our search of the area after the incident, we found the bodies of fifteen Mujis several miles east of the ambush site. From the looks of their wounds, they had been let out on the ground and then gunned down by one of the helicopters. Hinds, I believe you call them."

"That's also very convenient. You guys have covered your tracks pretty well."

Price decided that she had better step in between the two men to get this briefing away from personalities and back onto the facts. The President had ordered them to cooperate fully with Klimov, and cooperate they would.

"What is your analysis of this incident?" she asked.

"There are those in Russian Intelligence who think that the warheads are destined for certain of the radical Islamic terrorist groups. Some think that Saddam Hussein is making a serious bid to regain his power in the Gulf region. Others want to point the finger at Colonel Khaddafi."

"What do you think?" Price asked.

"I think that the North Koreans are involved," Klimov stated flatly. "And I think that they have joined up with the hard-liners in China in a plan to overthrow those who are trying to lead their countries to a capitalistic market economy."

"Why do you think that?"

The Russian smiled thinly. "I have spent my entire career working in the Far East bureau. I have seen the Chinese in action since the early Maoist days. I speak three dialects of their language, and I know how they think. You Americans seem to believe that the Chinese are going to follow the same road that we did, shake off Marx and Lenin and become good little capitalists. I, however, happen to know better.

"Even the so-called free-market Chinese leaders have the same mentality as the old hard-line Maoists did. They haven't given up their dreams of domination. All you have to do is look at what is going on in the Spratly Islands right now to see that."

The Spratly Islands were a widespread group of 105 rocky atolls and reefs between Vietnam and the Philippines that were claimed by both China and Vietnam. They were of no practical use to anyone, except for the fact that a Mobil oil-exploration team had found a huge deposit of gas and oil under them. The recent clashes between the Vietnamese and Chinese forces stationed there were being heralded as the next Far East flash point.

"So," Price stated, "assuming that your analysis is correct, what do you think they're going to do with the warheads?"

Klimov shrugged. "That, I don't know." He paused. "But, I can think of a dozen places where a two-kiloton nuclear warhead could cause a lot of trouble to the 'new world order,' as your President likes to call it."

"And kill a lot of people," Kurtzman added.

"As you are surely aware," Klimov went on, "the Chinese do not care all that much about people. They do care, however, about their place in the world. The death of several thousand people, even their own, is not of any great importance to them. Bringing the Pacific Rim under their political and economic control is, however."

"You think that they're going to use the warheads for nuclear blackmail."

"No, I think they are going to detonate them."

"But why?"

"For terrorism to be effective," he said with a shrug, "someone has to be killed. A threat is no good unless it is carried out."

"But why would they go to the trouble of hijacking Russian warheads then?" Kurtzman asked. "They have their own nukes and could use them if they wanted."

"But," Klimov replied, "if they use their own weapons, the West will be able to tie them to it through the detonation signatures. If they use our warheads, however, the detonation signatures will make the world believe that we did it. And we Russians will pay the price for something we didn't do. And, in the process, the hard-liners can use the turmoil as a cover for them to move to overthrow the 'free-market' leaders and take charge again."

Price turned to Kurtzman. "Aaron, who do we have on tap who can tell us something about the specifications of these weapons?"

Kurtzman thought for a moment. "Fielding, Dr. Richard Fielding at the Institute for Nuclear Studies in Denver. He's our best man on Russian tactical nuke systems."

"See if you can get him loaned to us for the duration of this operation," Price said.

"If the Man thinks that this is serious enough to send him here—" Kurtzman jerked a thumb toward Klimov "—I should have no trouble getting Fielding."

"In the meantime," Price said to the Russian, "let me see you to your room."

"Thank you," Klimov said.

"Don't thank me." She looked the man up and down slowly, thinking he looked more like a California lawyer than a Russian intelligence agent. He was wearing a tailored suit, a good watch, expensive shoes, and had a fresh haircut, and she didn't like him one bit. "I don't like your being here any more than Aaron does. But, around here, what the President says, goes.''

The Russian wisely kept his mouth shut as he followed Price down the hall. His own president had been equally emphatic about his cooperating fully with his old enemies. Klimov had always tried to keep his mind free of politics, and he had always followed orders like a good little Russian, no matter who it was giving them. That was the only way he had been able to make the transition from the KGB to the new Russian intelligence service. He was a rising star in the new system, and he wasn't about to make waves now.

CHAPTER THREE

Pusan, Korea

Mack Bolan ran flat out, driving his rubber-soled boots hard against the concrete of the loading dock as he dashed for cover in the deep shadows alongside the warehouse in front of him.

Reaching the building, he pressed his back against the corrugated sheet-metal wall and peered up at the darkened windows of the second-story offices. If his information was accurate, this was the hideout of the North Korean ninja team that had assassinated eight American businessmen in South Korea over the past several weeks.

The deaths attributed to this hit team hadn't been merely killings, they had been savage butchery. The victims—seven men, and one woman—had been brutally tortured and then further mutilated after death. Their bodies had been so horribly mangled that their positive identification had been possible only by checking the remains against their dental records.

Each of the bodies had been dumped in a prominent area of the city accompanied with a note in
English denouncing "American capitalistic neo-
imperialism." The notes also called upon the Korean workers to rid themselves of their "American
imperial slave masters" so they could regain control of their own destinies.

The notes were pure Marxist propaganda, but
they were effective. Particularly when they were
found in front of a hotel lobby attached to a naked,
butchered body. Many of the resident American
businessmen had taken extended leaves of absence
from their companies, and business travel from the
States was way down. Even tourist travel had suf-
fered.

The South Korean authorities had responded instantly to the terrorist attacks. The United States was
South Korea's biggest market partner, and anything that affected trade between the two countries
was critical. But, when they were unable to get a
handle on the situation themselves, they had asked
for help from America. Enter Mack Bolan, The
Executioner, and Phoenix Force, Stony Man Farm's
crack counterterrorist team.

By the time Bolan and Phoenix Force arrived to
take over the operation, the suspects had been ten-
tatively identified as a team of North Korean ninja
assassins. Once that was known, an all-out effort by

South Korean Intelligence came up with a tip from
a North Korean double agent. Now, Bolan and
Phoenix Force were closing in on the assassins. If
their information was correct, they would find them
in this empty warehouse at the end of a dock on the
Pusan harbor.

After assuring himself that his movement to the
warehouse had gone unnoticed, Bolan swung
around his 9 mm Heckler & Koch MP-5 submachine gun and signaled the rest of the team to move
in.

Calvin James was the first to reach his side. An
ex-Navy Seal by way of the mean streets of Chi-
cago, the lanky young black man was the newest
member of Phoenix Force. A knife fighter, para-
chutist, scuba diver, martial-arts and small-arms
expert, James also put his medical training to good
use as the team's medic.

James was followed quickly by David McCarter
and Gary Manning. McCarter was a Briton whose
easygoing, casual manner concealed a short-fused
temper and an attraction to danger. As far as he was
concerned, a life untested by constant brushes with
death was hardly worth living. When duty with the
SAS, the British Special Air Service, couldn't sat-
isfy his love of danger, he raced cars and flew anything with wings for amusement. When he'd been

offered a slot on the team, he had jumped at the chance.

Manning on the other hand, was a rugged and calm-natured Canadian who had been a lieutenant when offered the chance to be a "special observer" attached to the Fifth Special Forces in Vietnam. His extensive background in explosives had earned him a position on the squad as demolitions man.

The last man in the assault team, Rafael Encizo, slid in against the wall to join his comrades. A Cuban patriot who had been captured at the ill-fated invasion of the Bay of Pigs, he had survived the infamous prison on the Isle of Pines and welcomed the opportunity to become part of the Force.

The fifth man and leader of Phoenix Force, Yakov Katzenelenbogen, waited at the far end of the dock with the South Korean police reinforcements. The senior member of the team, the French-born Israeli began his life as a warrior while he was still a boy. Joining the fledgling Israeli army as soon as he was able, he had fought in dozens of campaigns until the Six-Day War when he lost his right arm to an antipersonnel mine. His next tour of duty was working counterterrorist operations for the Mossad, the Israeli intelligence service.

Having fought against terrorists all of his life and seeing the toll they had taken on innocent life, he had looked forward to working for Stony Man

Farm, an organization that wasn't hampered by politics or the law.

NOW THAT EVERYONE was in place, the Executioner signaled to go for the entry. While Manning readied a small lock-smashing demolition charge, James reached past him, tried the doorknob and found it unlocked. This either wasn't the place they were looking for, or the assassins welcomed visitors.

One by one, the black-clad Stony Man warriors slipped into the silky darkness inside the warehouse. With their night-vision goggles in place, the interior was revealed in shades of eerie green. But except for scattered piles of shipping crates and packing debris, the building appeared to be deserted. Even Manning's audio amplifier failed to pick up the normal sounds of sleeping men. It was possible that their information was wrong, or that the assassins were out on another mission.

After thoroughly scanning the apparently empty interior, Bolan signaled the others to move out. Even if no one was home, if they could find evidence that this was indeed the terrorists' hideout, they would stake it out until their quarry returned.

Bolan slowly walked out into the middle of the open floor. He checked out a small pile of shipping crates to his right, and when they showed nothing, he moved on. Poised on the balls of his feet, he sensed, more than saw, movement behind him and spun to confront it.

Only the swish of a sword blade cutting through the still air warned him of danger. Instinctively he swept up the barrel of his subgun to block the blow. The force of the blade against the barrel knocked the weapon from his hands.

Staggering backward, he cleared his .44 Magnum Desert Eagle automatic from leather with one smooth move and triggered a round at the dark shape in front of him.

The heavy slug drilled the ninja's throat and shattered his spine at the base of his skull, punching him to the floor, dead.

"Go! Go! Go!" Bolan yelled into his throat mike as he rushed past the Korean's corpse.

The detonation of a flash-bang grenade behind him threw the inside of the warehouse into harsh white light and black shadow. His night-vision goggles automatically blanked to shield his eyes from the glare.

When the goggles cleared a split second later, he saw another black-clad shape coming at him, a bright arc of steel flashing in his hand.

Bolan didn't know why the assassins had chosen to fight with swords, but that was all right with him. A .44 Magnum pistol round traveled faster than any sword he had ever seen.

He triggered the powerful Israeli-made pistol, and a 240-grain slug hammered his attacker in the chest. The Ninja staggered backward from the blow. But to Bolan's surprise, he recovered and charged again.

Modern body armor and ancient swords was an unusual combination, but Bolan didn't flinch. His second round took the North Korean in the middle of the forehead, blowing his brains out the back of his shattered skull.

This time, the ninja went down, his sword clattering to the concrete floor when it fell from his suddenly nerveless hands.

A short burst of autofire to his right, followed by a scream, told the warrior that someone else had also learned that using ancient swords against modern firearms hadn't been a wise choice.

The third ninja Bolan encountered was more up to date. The AKM assault rifle in his hands blazed 7.62 mm rounds on full-auto. The Executioner ducked for cover behind a concrete pillar, the bullets sending fragments of concrete into his face.

To Bolan's left, Manning spun and unleashed a short burst of return fire at his comrade's attacker. Though he missed, it caused the ninja to pause for a split second, which allowed Bolan to step out from cover and trigger two more rounds. The heavy slugs hammered the North Korean down to his knees.

To his right, Bolan heard James's battle cry and the stutter of another AKM. A return burst of 9 mm rounds and a muffled cry of pain ended the assault rifle's chatter. That was at least four down. How many more of them were out there?

Scanning the interior, all he could see were the dark green shapes of his own men. Manning and Encizo had teamed up, but McCarter and James were still hunting alone. The building looked to be clear, but Bolan's heightened combat senses still perceived danger.

He keyed his throat mike. "Calvin," he whispered, "I'm moving up on your left."

"I got you."

Without warning, a dark shape fell from the rafters onto James's back.

Bolan sighted in on the two men, but wasn't able to take the shot. Hearing a noise, he glanced up just in time to catch a flash of movement as another ninja dropped to the floor.

"They're above us!" he shouted, throwing himself out of the way.

The ninja landed lightly on his feet, swinging his AKM into target acquisition. Before he could bring it to bear, Bolan triggered two quick shots. The first two slugs hammered the North Korean backward, but a third was needed to put him down.

The warrior dropped to one knee to change magazines as gunfire broke out all around him. Working the pistol's slide to chamber a round, he looked back to see if James still needed help. The ex-Seal was out of trouble, but there was no shortage of targets now. At least half a dozen figures had dropped onto the floor, their AKMs blazing fire.

A lone figure raced toward the stairs at the far side of the building leading up to the building's second-floor office. Taking a two-handed stance, Bolan triggered three quick shots and was rewarded by seeing his target crumple ten feet from the bottom of the stairs.

The last ninja on his feet drew his sword, and, holding it high over his head, charged straight at Calvin James.

"He's mine!" the ex-Seal called as he took out his attacker with a short burst.

The last shot echoed away. When it was followed only by silence, Bolan keyed his throat mike. "Report!"

"Clear."

"All clear."

"Yo."

"Clear, Striker."

"We're all clear." Bolan flipped up his night-vision goggles. "Somebody find the light switch."

CHAPTER FOUR

When the lights came on, eleven black-clad bodies littered the floor of the warehouse. None of them showed signs of life, but the Stony Man team left nothing to chance. They quickly checked each one of the corpses to confirm the kills.

"Okay, Katz," Bolan radioed to Yakov Katzenelenbogen, who waited outside with the South Korean police reinforcements. "We're clear in here. Let them in."

"We're on the way. Is everyone all right?" he added. Katz had hated having to wait outside while the others cleaned out this nest of vipers, but someone had needed to stay with the reinforcements, and this time Katz was it.

"David has a couple of new dents in his body armor, but other than that, we're okay."

Katz reached down, picked up one of the ninjas' swords and tested the edge. "How many of them did you get?"

"We've counted eleven."

"Do you think that's all of them?"

"That's the leader and the two five-man hit teams we were told to expect."

"I'm glad this is over," the Israeli said, placing the sword back on the floor. "This was a nasty business."

The South Korean police quickly took charge of the lifeless bodies. One by one, they were photographed and fingerprinted before being slid into body bags and carried outside to begin the journey to the morgue.

While that was going on, another team of South Koreans started going through the papers they had found in the small second-level office. From the looks of the place, the ninjas had been in residence for several weeks.

"Colonel Pollock," the Korean interpreter called out, using the pseudonym Bolan had chosen for the mission, "I've found something I think you might be interested in seeing."

Bolan looked at the papers he was handed. They were covered with Korean characters and had a red ink stamp, a chop, at the bottom beside a scrawled ink signature.

"This says that the North Korean murderers were ordered to be out of Pusan by no later than the day after tomorrow."

"Does it say why?"

"No. It says only that it is essential that they be at least fifty kilometers away by that time. Even if their mission was not complete, they were to pull out anyway."

Bolan frowned. "Is there anything special planned in the city on that date?"

The Korean cop thought for a moment. "Not that I can think of." He paused. "Except that a North Korean delegation is arriving for the big trade show next week. We have been alerted to provide extra security for them."

"What trade show?"

"There is a five-day economic conference and trade show going on this week. Delegates are coming from all over the Pacific Rim trading nations."

"And the North Koreans are attending?"

"For the first time, yes."

Even though there had been no weakening of the iron-fisted Communist regime in North Korea, they had seen the free-market handwriting on the wall. They realized the value of opening trade with the capitalist Republic of South Korea and wanted to get it started.

Since they didn't have a hard currency that could be traded in the world's money markets, the North Koreans could never be a major economic player. But, even if they couldn't replace the United States, Japan or Taiwan as one of South Korea's major trading partners, they hoped to offer cheap raw materials to the South in return for badly needed manufactured consumer goods. It would be a small beginning, but it would be something for them to start building a real economy on.

"Can you get me a translation of that in the morning?" Bolan asked.

"No problem, Colonel."

Bolan called Katzenelenbogen over and explained what the Korean interpreter had told him. "What do you make of something like that?"

The gruff Israeli thought for a moment. There was only one reason he could think of for that kind of order to have been given. But no, the idea was too farfetched. If this was Israel and the North Koreans were fanatic death-seeking Shiite terrorists, he could believe the unthinkable. But, this was the Far East, not the Middle East. Yet, all of the right pieces were in place for the unthinkable to happen.

"You have something, Katz?" Bolan asked when he saw the expression on the ex-Mossad agent's face.

"I don't know," he said slowly. "It only makes sense if their mission controllers had something planned for the city and didn't want their team to get caught up in it. Something terrible."

"A nuclear detonation?"

Katz nodded.

"It's got all the earmarks," Bolan agreed. "But does anyone have any nuclear weapons missing?"

With the breakup of the old Soviet Union, control of the world's nuclear-weapon arsenal had become considerably more complicated. Over the past three years, several weapons had been stolen and sold on the international arms black market. Each one had been recovered in time, but nuclear missiles falling into the wrong hands was still a serious threat to world peace that had to be constantly guarded against.

"None that I know of, but you will have to ask Aaron about that when you talk to him."

"I will. As soon as we get back to the base."

IT WAS ANOTHER HOUR before the warehouse cleanup was completed. After a final check with the police, Bolan and Phoenix Force were driven back to the U.S. Air Force base outside the city. Since they were in Korea on an officially sanctioned mission this time, they had been using the base as their staging area. It gave them ready access to any supplies and equipment they might need, as well as providing a worldwide communication capability.

The first thing Bolan did was to go to the base communications center to get a secure line back to Barbara Price at Stony Man to report the success of the mission. Also, he wanted to talk to Aaron

Kurtzman about the cryptic North Korean orders they had found in the warehouse and ask about missing nuke weapons.

With his cover as Colonel Rance Pollock on a special mission for the President, he had no trouble getting access to a secure channel back to the States. In fact, his cover documents gave him and his men instant access to anything on the base.

"You're up late, Colonel," one of the Air Force comtechs greeted him. "You want your usual line?"

Bolan nodded and picked up the red phone.

Stony Man Farm

STONY MAN FARM WAS buzzing when Bolan's call came in. With the President's authority having cleared the way, Aaron Kurtzman was filtering and collating intelligence input from over a dozen sources. The CIA, the Israeli Mossad, Britain's MI-6, Russian Intelligence, the French and the Japanese were all feeding their agent reports directly into his computer center. He was even receiving spotty feed from the Turks and Egyptians.

However, no one had come up with a lead on the missing warheads yet. Because of the location of the heist, most of the efforts to locate them were being concentrated in the Middle East. Hundreds of agents were in the field, and both recon aircraft and satellites were probing the earth below, but nothing was turning up.

Klimov's belief that the North Koreans or the Chinese had been behind the hijackers wasn't getting much play with most of the world's intelligence services. Except, of course, for the Japanese, Australians and South Koreans. If the Russian's assumption was correct, they were the most likely terrorist targets for the stolen warheads.

Almost everyone else was betting that the missing weapons would turn up in one of the Middle East terrorist camps. The lull in terrorist activity that had immediately followed Operation Desert Storm had ended. Although the major organizations were cut off from their old sources of arms and finances, they had resurfaced to continue their activities. Also, they had now been joined by newly formed groups, mostly Kurds and Shiites, that had been born from the aftermath of the short Gulf War.

Since any of them would go to any lengths to get their hands on a nuclear warhead, the camps were being closely watched by every means known to intelligence gathering. Every time that one of the would-be "international freedom fighters" walked to the slit latrines to relieve himself, someone was watching and logging it. If they had their bloody hands on the missing weapons, they would be found.

Bolan's call was a welcome break for Price, and his report of the successful conclusion of the mission was just what she needed to hear. It was nice to know that one of their operations was going well. The secretary of trade had been particularly concerned about this situation. In the current uncertain economic times, anything that upset the American balance of trade was of immediate concern.

The Executioner told Price about the assassins' orders to evacuate Pusan. "And," he concluded, "Katz is concerned. He wants me to ask if anyone is missing any nuclear weapons that we don't know about."

"Striker," Price replied, her voice suddenly becoming tense, "yesterday we were alerted to a situation that you're not aware of. There *are* some nukes missing. A week ago, the Russians lost a convoy of ten tactical nuclear warheads along the Kazakhstan border. We also have reason to believe that either the Chinese or the North Koreans could have been involved in the hijacking."

There was a long silence on the other end of the secure line. "That would fit," Bolan finally said. "And we all have to be concerned with the possibility of nuclear terrorism. Why else would the North Koreans have ordered their assassins to evacuate the town? What's the status on this situation right now?"

"On the President's orders, we're working with the Russians on this one. And the Man's putting a lot of pressure on keeping this contained and out of the press. He has everyone from the CIA to Interpol working overtime on finding those warheads. Hal's been on the horn to us every hour, wanting to know if we've gotten anything yet. He'll be glad to get your intel. It's our first real lead."

She paused. "Since you're on the scene, I'll tell him that you'll follow up on it. Is there anything you'll need?"

"If Katz's hunch is right and there's a nuke coming in on that North Korean ship, I'll need a nuclear ordnance disposal team and all the information we can get on those Russian warheads ASAP."

"No problem with that. I'll get them on their way as soon as you hang up."

"As far as the rest of it, we have enough equipment left over from the ninja mission. Anything else we need, I can get from the Air Force here."

"Roger. Shout if there's anything we can do to help out."

"What are the Russians doing to get their missing items back?"

"Well, the first thing they did was send us a liaison officer."

"How did the Bear take that?"

"About as well as you can expect."

Price didn't have to elaborate. Bolan understood only too well. The only attack on Stony Man Farm that had even come close to succeeding had been launched by the KGB. In the desperate battle, Aaron Kurtzman had sustained the bullet wounds that had put him in a wheelchair for the rest of his life.

"Then, just to make matters worse," Price continued, "this particular man was the KGB officer responsible for the Soviet interrogation of our POWs in Vietnam."

The Executioner was silent for a moment as he remembered the men still missing in action. The Vietnam MIA-POW issue was still an open, bleeding wound in the American psyche and one that would be slow to heal, if it ever did. Every new revelation about the fate of the missing men only caused the blood to flow anew.

He could well understand Kurtzman's anger; he felt the same anger himself. But this was a new era. Enemies, as well as friends, changed with time, and if an old enemy could help stop this latest nuclear threat, he was welcome.

"Tell Bear to calm down and milk this guy for everything we can get from him. We might need the information sometime in the future."

"I've got him working on it already, but our man is being very careful. He reveals only what we need to know to deal with this particular crisis."

"Keep on him and make sure you're taping everything he says," Bolan suggested. "But he shouldn't press the guy too hard. If he's on the level, we'll need his help. We don't want to get him angry."

"I'll keep an eye on Aaron."

"It's too late to start working on this tonight," Bolan said. "And I need to get at least a couple of hours' sleep before I start. Get those support people on the way over here and try to get me an appointment to talk to Korean Intelligence about this first thing in the morning. In the meantime, if you get anything new, fax it to me here."

"Will do. Be careful, Striker." Bolan could hear the concern in her voice.

"Careful's my middle name."

"Yeah, right."

CHAPTER FIVE

Stony Man Farm

Even with the presidential authority speeding things along, it was still several hours before Dr. Richard Fielding could be flown from his Denver research center to the Farm. The first thing he did after he arrived was listen, over a cup of coffee, to Klimov's theory about the theft of the warheads.

"It's an interesting theory, I admit," Fielding stated, carefully setting his cup down as soon as the Russian had finished speaking. The last thing he wanted to do was to spill any of the too-strong brew on himself. "It's too bad that it's wrong."

"Exactly what do you mean by that, Dick?" Kurtzman asked.

"This particular piece of Soviet hardware," he explained, "the RK-36 warhead, just happens to be a design that's been around for years. It's a rather simple single-stage nonboosted plutonium implosion weapon. The Chinese copied it years ago for their Silkworm and Flying Dragon attack missiles.

If one of these things goes off, the Chinese are as likely to be blamed for it as the Russians."

Kurtzman slowly turned his wheelchair around to lock eyes with the Russian. "Well, Colonel, what do you have to say about that?"

The intelligence officer shrugged. "Even if what Dr. Fielding says is true, it doesn't mean that my government is behind some kind of plot to blackmail the world with nuclear weapons."

"But it does put you guys back in the running, though, doesn't it?" Kurtzman wasn't smiling. "What you said about the hard-core Chinese not wanting to give up on Marxism also goes for some of you Russians, doesn't it? From what I understand, there's a strong cadre of senior officers who want to see their president fall on his ass so they can have an excuse to take over and go back to the glory days."

Kurtzman's jab was much too close to the mark for Klimov to protest. One of the areas he had been concentrating on before this incident came up was trying to counter military-led conspiracies to overthrow the civilian regime. And there had been more than the one well-publicized plot against Gorbachev to deal with.

"Let me get in contact with my people," he asked Barbara Price, "and I will try to confirm this weapons information for you. I am not a nuclear-weapons expert, and we cannot afford to make a mistake at this point because I didn't give you the correct information about it."

He nodded toward Fielding. "And if it is as the good doctor here has said, then I will have to re-think this affair."

"You'd better think pretty damned fast," Kurtz-man said. "The first time one of those things goes off, you people are going to be in deep shit."

Price turned to face Kurtzman. "If the North Koreans *are* involved, maybe we can pick up some echoes of it in the West Coast Korean community. Do you have anything new out there?"

Both Price and Kurtzman were well aware that the Asian Communist nations had sent hundreds of agents to the United States in the guise of immi-grants. Some of them reported back on the activi-ties of their dissident countrymen, some of them joined Asian gangs to provide hard currency for their homelands, while others simply spied and gathered data. All of them, however, were good sources of information about what was going on in their home governments.

"The only thing I've been seeing lately is that the Vietnamese and Korean gangs seemed to have de-clared a complete cease-fire all up and down the coast."

"Why have they done that?" Price asked. "I thought they were in the middle of a new drug-turf war."

"No one seems to know." Kurtzman shrugged. "But the body count has been way down lately. Last weekend, there were no Asian gang casualties in all of L.A."

"Who can we use to look into this?"

Kurtzman punched a code into his keyboard, and the monitor lighted up with a profile of all the Asian-American federal agents working on the West Coast Asian gang situation. He quickly scrolled through the list until he found the name he was looking for.

"We don't have any Korean-Americans on tap," he said. "But I've got a guy in Seattle, a Vietnamese-American named Le Van Pham who's running the DEA's West Coast Asian Gang Task Force. He's been helpful to us in the past, he's cleared to the highest levels and he's well connected all the way down to San Diego. I can give him a call and see if he's available to help us with this."

Price thought for a moment. "Do that. But make sure that you don't mention what we're looking for. The President has been emphatic about none of this reaching the press. Tell him that we're sending a team up there and they'll brief him in person. Able

Team's got that Texas operation just about wrapped up."

Kurtzman snorted. "They'll probably enjoy the change of scenery. Gadgets has been complaining about the heat ever since they got there."

"See how close they are to finishing up down there," she said. "Then give them their marching orders."

"It's as good as done."

"In the meantime," she said, turning to Dr. Fielding, "I'd like to get some damage estimates on what those warheads can do so we have a better idea of what we're working with here."

Mercedes, Texas

CARL "IRONMAN" LYONS lay in the Texas dust on a slight rise in the ground that overlooked a small deserted dirt airstrip outside of Mercedes. This was cotton country. The rich, flat acreage of the Rio Grande valley stretched for miles, growing the big-bole fluffy Texas cotton that would become next year's Levi's jeans and Jockey underwear. The short runway and the dirt road leading to it had been scraped out of the tilled land.

The airfield had supposedly been built to service the crop-duster planes that kept the bole weevils under control. One of the ugly but functional Grumman Ag Cat duster planes sat in the sun beside the shack that stored the sacks of pesticide it would spray on the crops. The plane was as dusty and disreputable as the rest of the field, but the fresh oil dripping from the engine cowling showed that it had been flown recently.

"This had better work," Lyons growled to the man lying in the dust beside him, monitoring a radio link.

Lyons was big and blond, an ex-LAPD cop whose path had crossed that of Executioner Mack Bolan's during the Mafia wars. Now he was part of Stony Man, heading Able Team, which was targeted at domestic terrorism and violence. His nickname "Ironman" came from his determined way of dealing with the obstacles, both physical and mental, that life threw in his path.

"It'll work, Ironman," the man with the radio, Hermann Schwarz, assured him. "Our information is good. They'll be here before too much longer."

Schwarz was a lean man with salt-and-pepper hair cut short in military fashion. He was known as "Gadgets" because of his skill with anything mechanical or electronic, a nickname he had picked up in Vietnam because of his work with booby traps and surveillance devices.

"What's your status, Gadgets?" The voice of Rosario Blancanales, the other third of Lyons's Able Team, came over Schwarz's earphone.

Known as the "Politician" because of his unique ability to work people and situations to his advantage, the Puerto Rican was working as their liaison with the federal agencies and the Texas Rangers on this operation.

"We're still collecting fire ants and working on our tans," Schwarz replied.

"I hope this goes down today so we can wrap this up quick. I just got a call from the Bear, and Barb's got a hot one for us. She wants us to drop everything and get to Seattle ASAP."

"What's up?"

"He didn't say."

Schwarz wasn't surprised to hear that. Even with the portable secure communications gear they had with them, Kurtzman was always reluctant to give too much classified information over the airwaves. When they arrived at SeaTac airport outside of Seattle, a Justice Department courier would be waiting for them with a mission packet.

Schwarz mopped his damp forehead with his sleeve. After five hours in the blazing Rio Grande sun, he was surprised that he could still sweat. The Kevlar vest he wore under his pearl-buttoned Western shirt was baking him like a Thanksgiving turkey.

"Seattle will be lovely this time of year," he said wistfully. "Lots of nice tall trees with nice cool shade under them and a cool breeze blowing in from the sound."

"Can it, guys!" Lyons cut in on the comlink chatter. "We've got company."

Schwarz tilted his cowboy hat back and brought his field glasses to his eyes. An older, red Cadillac convertible with two male passengers was winding its way up the dirt road. Following in the Caddy's dust plume was a new, white Ford one-ton pickup truck with three men in the cab and a canvas cover over a load of something in the bed.

The Able Team warrior reached down and brought up the Sony video camera with the telephoto zoom lens. The Feds wanted this drop on tape so some bleeding-heart defense lawyer couldn't scream "entrapment" when the case went to court.

The Caddy braked to a dusty halt in front of the small control shack at the end of the airstrip while the pickup drove over to the Ag Cat crop duster. Three men in blue jeans, T-shirts, hats and cowboy boots got out of the truck and ripped the canvas off the rear of the truck.

"Bingo," Schwarz said when he saw the eighty-pound paper bags of pesticide stacked in the truck bed. "It's going down."

As the two Able Team warriors watched, the three men tore open the sacks and started to pour the white powder they contained into the hopper on the Ag Cat.

"You getting all this?" Lyons asked.

"Damned straight," Schwarz replied without looking up. "In sound and living color. The only way this sucker could get any better would be if I had 3-D and stereo sound. Justice is going to love this. These guys won't have a chance in court."

The stakeout was the culmination of a long investigation of a Mexican agricultural chemical company believed to be involved in cocaine smuggling. Owned by a Mexican police official already under investigation, the company had come under suspicion when it had run afoul of the tax man. It was soon discovered that the books showed assets much greater than the profits from selling pesticides to cotton farmers in northern Mexico and south Texas could possibly warrant.

The problem was that if the company was a front for drug smuggling, no one had been able to discover how the drugs were being smuggled into the United States. The company itself had been raided several times, but nothing had been found. The company's trucks had been stopped and their cargo inspected, but nothing other than pesticide had ever been found. Then, an American pilot had been apprehended in another drug case.

In exchange for lenience, he had explained how the cocaine was packaged in pesticide bags and sent across the border in previously inspected truck shipments. Then, it was taken to this small airstrip close to the Mexican border, loaded into the crop dusters and flown to other destinations for distribution.

It was an intricate operation, but now Schwarz had it all on tape. He had the bags with the chemical-company logo on them, he had the licence plates of the vehicles, the FAA registration number on the plane and the faces of the men. These guys were looking at twenty years minimum in a federal prison when the videotapes reached the DEA regional office in Dallas. All that was left now was to follow the Ag Cat to see where it delivered the cocaine it carried.

That was Blancanales's part of the operation. He was two miles away, sitting on the ground in a DEA helicopter waiting to follow the Ag Cat when it took off. The chopper was equipped with a sophisticated air-to-air radar and a full electronics suite so it could track the plane without being spotted. Texas Ranger and federal ground units had been alerted all over the state so that no matter where the small plane set down, someone would be waiting to greet it and the cargo it carried.

The two men who had arrived in the Caddy leaned against the car's fender and smoked while the other men filled the plane's hoppers. As soon as the hoppers were full, they were closed and one of the men from the Caddy stepped into the small shack. When he came out, he was wearing a one-piece flight suit complete with leather helmet and flying goggles, a drug-smuggling Red Baron.

Climbing up into the cockpit of the Ag Cat, the pilot engaged the starter and the big radial engine started with a belch of smoke and a coughing roar as the propeller started to spin. Running the engine up, the pilot kicked the rudder over to hard left and stood on the left-rudder pedal brake to turn the plane into the wind.

"Get ready, Pol," Schwarz said. "It's going down."

"Roger. We've got the rotor turning."

With its exhaust stack bellowing, the crop duster headed down the airstrip. In less than a hundred yards, its wheels were off the ground and it started to climb out over the cotton fields.

"He's headed northeast on a bearing of zero six three," Schwarz said.

"Roger," Blancanales acknowledged. "We're picking up his transponder now."

The first thing Lyons and Schwarz had done when they arrived at the airstrip early that morning had been to hide a small transponder in the plane, set to go on when the engine was started.

"Don't lose him."

"Don't worry," the Puerto Rican reassured him. "He hasn't got a chance."

When Schwarz raised the videocamera again, the lens caught the light.

The driver of the Caddy saw the flash of the sun off the lens. "Somebody's over there!" he shouted, pointing to the Able Team warrior's hiding place. "Get 'em, boys!"

CHAPTER SIX

At the smuggler's shout, the two Able Team warriors sprang into action. Caught out in the open as they were, their only chance to live was to fight.

"Oh, shit!" Schwarz muttered as he dived for the 9 mm H&K MP-5 submachine gun in the dirt beside him. He had hoped that they could pull off this little number without a confrontation. It was too damned hot for a firefight, but here it was.

Beside him, Lyons brought up his SPAS-12 assault shotgun and clicked the full-auto 12-gauge street sweeper off safe. Their four-wheel-drive pickup was parked out of sight in the fields well over a mile away, so there was no way they could get back to it without being seen. They were simply not going to get away from this one today without a battle.

But that was fine with the Ironman. The odds they were facing weren't all that bad—there were only the five smugglers. It had to be at least five to one before things were serious. If these guys wanted to get nasty about it, he would be more than happy to accommodate whatever they had in mind. Drug

smugglers were real low on the short list of his fa-
vorite people.

The Caddy driver dived into the front seat of his
car and came up with a little 9 mm chopper in his
hands spitting flame. The muzzle climb of the
subgun sent the rounds singing high over their
heads.

For some unfathomable reason Schwarz could
never understand, drug runners usually went for
flashy, short-ranged, inaccurate weapons. Didn't
they know that one well-aimed shot was worth more
than two dozen rounds sprayed around the general
vicinity?

Sighting in carefully, Schwarz ripped off a pre-
cise, 6-round burst from his MP-5. None of the
slugs found a home, but they sent the smugglers
scrambling for cover behind their vehicles and let
them know their enemies meant business.

Lyons's SPAS roared, sending a blast of 12-gauge
Magnum-powered buckshot splattering into the side
of the red Caddy convertible. His shot was answered by a hail of return fire from the smugglers
that kept both of the Able Team warriors flat on
their faces in the dust. There was no cover anywhere in their vicinity, and to get up and run was
sure death.

The only thing they could do was to hug the dirt
and shoot it out.

With the five smugglers well under cover now, they took turns keeping up a steady barrage of lead.

While the Caddy driver and two of his men kept Lyons and Schwarz pinned down, the other two smugglers tried to go out through the cotton field to outflank them on the right. It was something that might look good in the movies, but it was a bad tactical move in this particular situation.

There was no real concealment in the knee-high cotton plants, and Lyons spotted the men the instant they broke cover. Keeping low, they dashed a hundred yards out into the field before turning back toward the two Able Team warriors.

"Keep them busy!" Lyons shouted over the roar of gunfire as he turned. "I'll take care of these two!"

Assuming a prone firing position facing the cotton field, Lyons watched the two cowboys make their approach. They'd had some kind of military training at one time because one of them would fire a burst from his subgun while the other one ran forward a few yards.

Fire and movement it was called. But for it to work, you had to be able to shoot straight. And with the small 9 mm subguns they carried, Lyons knew they couldn't hit the broad side of a barn if they were standing in front of it.

While Schwarz kept up the fire, Lyons patiently waited until the lead man of the pair was only a hundred yards away. That was about the maximum range for his shotgun, but he was confident he could make the shot. Slugs from the smugglers' subguns sang overhead and chewed into the Texas dirt around him, but he ignored them as he took careful aim. When the charging cowboy completely filled his sights, he triggered the SPAS.

The big gun roared, and the Magnum-powered load of double-aught buckshot caught the man square in the middle of the chest. The twelve .36-caliber lead balls tore open his rib cage, exposing the lungs and heart underneath. The force of the blow stopped the smuggler in his tracks, and he crumpled to the ground, dead.

The other cowboy took a quick look at the bloodied mess that had been his buddy and abruptly changed direction. Dropping his weapon, he sprinted as fast as he could through the cotton field, his boot heels throwing up little spurts of dust as he ran.

Lyons let him go and returned to the three men still at the airstrip. When one of them stood to take better aim with his subgun, Schwarz took him out with a burst to the chest. The man threw his arms up and toppled over, his weapon falling from his hands.

Seeing the flank attack fail, the Caddy driver vaulted over the passenger side of his vehicle and tried to make a run for it. Spraying lead from the submachine gun with his off hand, he started the big V-8 engine. When the engine caught, he slammed the gearshift into low range, cranked the steering wheel over as hard as he could and stood on the throttle.

The Caddy surged forward, its spinning wheels sending up twin clouds of dust as the back end slid sideways under the sudden acceleration. As the car took off, the driver held his trigger down, spraying 9 mm slugs at his adversaries.

Rolling away from the gunfire, Lyons came up with the assault shotgun in his hands roaring and spitting flame. The first shot peppered the door and shattered the windshield. The second load of buckshot took the driver in the side of the head and shoulders, slamming him forward against the dashboard.

The subgun fell from his hand, and, with a dead driver at the wheel, the convertible rammed the control shack, breaking through the door. The heavy car came to a halt halfway inside. Its engine was still running at half throttle with a dead foot on the gas pedal, its rear tires digging twin ruts in the rich Texas soil.

The last man on his feet raced for the Ford pickup, firing his subgun wildly. Rising up to his knees, Schwarz calmly aimed and triggered a 3-round burst that ended the gunner's attempt at a getaway. The man went down in midstride. Rolling over onto his back, he raised both his arms in a sign of surrender.

As suddenly as it had began, the fight was over.

"Cover me!" Lyons said as he drew his .357 Colt Python from his shoulder holster and stood up.

"Right." Schwarz sighted his MP-5 in as Lyons cautiously moved down to clear the killing zone.

After kicking their weapons out of the reach of the two wounded smugglers, Lyons bound their wrists behind their backs with plastic restraints.

"Mister," the first man pleaded as Lyons bent over him, "please help me, I'm bleeding."

"Tough. You won't die." Lyons snarled, as he jerked the restraint tight over his wrists. His job was to neutralize the smugglers, not to patch them up. The Feds could do that if they wanted to, but he sure as hell wasn't going to.

When the wounded man had been secured, he walked over to where the Caddy convertible was still trying its best to drive through the remains of the wooden shack. Reaching in over the corpse of the driver, he turned the ignition key to switch off the engine.

In the sudden silence, Lyons could hear sirens wailing in the distance. The cavalry was coming after the fight was all over. But that was all right with him. Had they been here, he and Schwarz would have had to play the game by the legalistic rules, which could easily have gotten one of them killed. Working alone, Able Team had once again dispensed instant justice to those who needed it.

The Caddy driver was dead behind the wheel of his flashy convertible. The two men who had stayed with him were both seriously wounded. The smuggler who had led the flank attack was dead. The only one to have escaped unhurt was the guy who was still running across the open cotton fields.

When the first federal car braked to a halt, Schwarz walked over and handed the videocamera to the DEA agent who stepped out of the passenger side.

"It's all in here," the Able Team warrior told him. "Everything from the time they drove up until the plane took off."

"Great," the Fed said. "Did you tape the firefight?"

"Sorry." Schwarz shook his head. "We were a bit busy at the time."

The agent glanced over at the body bags being laid out and the paramedics who were busy patching up the two wounded smugglers.

"You only got four out of the five? You boys are losing your touch."

Like most of the law-enforcement officers who occasionally came into contact with Able Team, the agent envied the extralegal authority that allowed them to deal instant justice from a blazing muzzle.

"We let the other one get away." Schwarz shrugged. "He dropped his gun and beat feet."

"Don't worry," the agent said with a grin. "We spotted him, and a chopper is closing in on him right now."

"They'd better hurry before he reaches El Paso. That guy's really moving."

"He can't outrun a chopper."

ROSARIO BLANCANALES arrived back at the airstrip in the DEA helicopter an hour and a half later. He had a big grin on his face as he stepped out onto the ground and shot his partners a thumbs-up.

"We got them," he stated. "When the Ag Cat set down at a little dirt airstrip outside of Beeville, the Texas Rangers were waiting for him. They got the pilot and the guys waiting for the delivery. The good news is that this thing's all wrapped up."

"If that's the good news," Schwarz asked, "what's the bad news?"

"The Bear wants us in Seattle ASAP."

"Don't we even get a little R and R after finishing up this gig?"

The Puerto Rican shook his head. "Nope. He's got the tickets waiting for us in San Antonio, and he wants us out of here. This is a hot one."

"What's going down?" Lyons asked.

"He didn't say. All he said was for us to get there as fast as we could."

Schwarz wiped his sleeve across his face. "Then I guess we'd better kiss this oven goodbye. You know how cranky the Bear can get when we're late for a party." He sighed dramatically. "I was kind of looking forward to a little time off in an air-conditioned hotel room, but at least it'll be nice and cool in Seattle."

Lyons smiled secretly. He knew better. It would be cool in Seattle, all right. But in the spring, Seattle could also be the wettest place on earth. He knew that Schwarz hated rain even more than he did the heat.

He clapped the smaller man on the shoulder. "You'll love Seattle, Gadgets. I promise."

"I'm looking forward to it."

CHAPTER SEVEN

Pusan AFB, Korea

The Korean CIA liaison man arrived early to report to the secure briefing room in the Air Force base operations building. Though they'd had little sleep since the late-night mission against the ninjas, Mack Bolan and the other Stony Man warriors were well fortified with coffee and were waiting to meet him.

"Colonel Rance Pollock," Bolan introduced himself, extending his hand.

"Kim Tae Ro, Republic of Korea Intelligence."

Kim was tall for a Korean. But then, he was young enough to have benefited from the improved diet of the postwar era. When the Korean shook his hand, Bolan could feel the hardened calluses that marked hands well practiced in the martial arts. He wasn't surprised. The Koreans had always trained their soldiers in the ancient combat techniques as well as with modern weaponry. He would have been more surprised if the Korean hadn't been trained.

Kim felt the same hard-earned calluses on Bolan's hand, and his respect for the American instantly went up several notches. Most of the American military men he had worked with had the soft hands of shopkeepers. This man's hand felt like that of a sensei, a master of the martial arts.

There was something about the colonel's cold blue eyes and stance, as well, that spoke of his being a human weapon. Kim momentarily wondered how the American would do against him on the practice field. He quickly banished the thought. This wasn't the kind of man one could have a friendly bout with. With him the potential was there for mortal combat.

When Bolan introduced him to the Phoenix Force commandos, Kim instantly saw that they were much like the colonel—professional warriors. Even the older man with the artificial arm had an aura of danger about him. The Korean had been a little skeptical at first, but now that he had met these new allies, he had no doubts that they could work together.

After offering Kim coffee, they got right down to business. "We received the information from your headquarters about the stolen Russian warheads yesterday," Kim said. "And after finding the document in the warehouse last night, we have put all of our agents in the North working on it."

"What have they learned so far?"

"Sadly nothing," the Korean agent answered. "But we lost two of our deep cover agents in Pyongyang early this morning when we activated them. They did not check back as required and we think they were compromised. The North Korean liaison bureau, their version of the KGB, is at a state of increased alert, so we do believe that something significant is going on."

"What is your analysis of the reason for ordering the North Korean assassins to be out of Pusan by tomorrow?" Bolan asked.

"We have gone over the document very carefully," Kim replied, "and we feel the same as your superiors do. In light of the stolen Russian warheads, we think that there is a very good chance that the North Korean ship bringing the trade delegation could have one of them on board."

"But would they sacrifice their own delegation that way?" Katzenelenbogen asked.

"Yes, they would," Kim replied emphatically. "As far as their party officials are concerned, the delegates are no more than glorified shopkeepers. Even though some of them are of ministerial rank, they have little value to the socialist state. Plus, if their own officials die in a nuclear blast, it will turn the blame away from themselves."

Of all of the Asian Communists, the North Koreans had always been the most brutal and the most willing to spend the lives of their people for political or propaganda gain. Bolan could well believe that they would use the lives of their own people once more to gain a propaganda victory while they were covering their tracks.

"The part of this I can't figure out," Katz said, "is why they would go to all of the trouble to set up this trade conference only to use it as a terrorist target."

"That is something we have no answer for," Kim admitted. "We are as puzzled by it as you are. It has taken months to put this together, and my government has seen it as a welcome sign of a softening in their attitudes. But now we do not know what to think. We simply do not know what they can possibly gain from this."

"Is it possible to deny the ship entry to the country?" Bolan asked, bringing the conversation back to the matter at hand. When this was all over, someone could take the time to analyze why it had been done. Right now, the only important thing was to stop the warhead from detonating and killing thousands of people.

"No," Kim stated bluntly. "The political situation does not allow us that option. This economic conference has been months in the planning, and it cannot be canceled without great loss of face for my government."

"Will the city be evacuated?"

"That, too, is something we cannot do. My government will not bow to Communist terrorism. If they do strike at us, we will retaliate. But we will not cower in front of them."

Though the governments of North and South Korea couldn't be any more different, the mind-set of their peoples was very similar. They both shared the same stubborn, fatalistic view of life that didn't allow for backing down in front of an enemy. If the North Koreans would send their trade delegation to certain death, the South Koreans would risk a city full of their own citizens rather than be seen as cowards.

"When is the ship due to dock?" Bolan asked, focusing again on the operational questions.

"It's scheduled to arrive this afternoon around 1600 hours. It was to have docked at the main port, but now when it comes in, it will be diverted to the south end of the harbor. That way it will be isolated, and we will be able to easily surround it."

The Korean paused. "But if the weapon goes off, it will not make much difference where it is docked."

"Which is why we have to find it before it does," Bolan said. "And with the deadline set for tomorrow, we have to take it out this evening. Since we don't know when it's going to be detonated, there's too great a risk if we wait until sometime tomorrow."

He turned to nod at Phoenix Force. "I don't know how your government plans to handle this, but you can consider us to be at your disposal for this operation."

"Thank you." Kim half bowed. "We have been told of your recent activities in the Middle East regarding nuclear weapons, and we value your expertise in this area. My government would be honored if you would lead this operation for us."

This was what the Stony Man team had been waiting to hear. Now they could get into gear, working to stop this new terrorist threat. Even though Americans weren't directly threatened this time, terrorism anywhere threatened free peoples all over the world. But with the deadline given in the captured documents, they had precious little time to put an operation together.

"We accept the job, but I don't have enough men to handle it alone. We'll need some help and support."

"I can offer you an English-speaking Korean special forces unit," Kim told him. "Twenty men trained by both your own Army's Delta Force and the British SAS."

"They should do nicely," Bolan said. "But we'll only need six men trained in counterterrorist tactics to go on board the ship with us."

"They will be here within the hour."

"Then, once we've located the warhead, we'll need a support team and an escort to transport it from the docks back here. I'm having a nuclear ordnance disposal team flown in from the States to take care of the weapon once we get our hands on it."

"I see no problem with any of that," Kim said as he took notes. "Is there anything else you will need?"

"We'll need a map of the harbor," Rafael Encizo spoke up. As the team's maritime expert, he would lead the search of the ship for the weapon. "And anything you can give us on the ship itself. Plans, photos, etcetera. The more we know about the target, the better our chances."

"I have a map of the dock area with me," the Korean replied, opening his briefcase. "And I will check on information about the ship. If we don't have anything on file, I can have the Korean air force fly a recon plane over it and take photographs for you."

"I'll need a radiac meter," Gary Manning said, "and a microcircuit tester." When the warhead was found, as the team's explosives expert, his job would be to render it safe enough that it could be moved back to the air base.

"I think we all could use lead-lined jockstraps," McCarter said, grinning. "No use in risking the family jewels, you know. Posterity and all that."

"There'll be more than the old family jewels in trouble if that thing goes off," James said grimly.

"That's why we have to find it before it goes off," Katz told them confidently.

As soon as the Korean agent left, Bolan and Katzenelenbogen got to work on the assault plan. Capturing a ship could be tricky, even when it was in port, and they didn't have time to set up anything complex. This was going to have to be a straightforward up-the-gangway-and-smash-their-way-on-board mission. Since the ship would have only one gangway leading from the dock to the deck, it would be a frontal assault.

When the Executioner and Katz had worked things out, Bolan called Barbara Price at the Farm and briefed her on the operations plan they had come up with. The Stony Man Farm staff then immediately went to work coordinating the mission support the warriors would need. A Russian nuclear weapons technician had to be rushed to Pusan along with an American nuclear ordnance disposal—NOD—team. Working under the Russian's supervision, the Americans would be responsible for dismantling the weapon once it had been recovered.

After lengthy consultation between Hal Brognola and the Oval Office, it was decided that the American air base wouldn't be evacuated. If the South Koreans were willing to trust the Stony Man warriors to be able to save Pusan from nuclear destruction, it wouldn't do not to have the Americans share the same fate. Even more important, however, was that any evacuation attempt would tip off the unknown terrorists that their plan had been discovered. That might make them detonate the bomb early, or take the ship back out to sea, and it was essential that the warhead be captured.

TRUE TO KIM'S WORD, a Korean special forces major and five soldiers showed up within the hour. The six men looked like they had all been punched out of the same mold. They were stocky, of medium height, with well-muscled bodies and hard hands. Short haircuts, camouflaged fatigues, spit-shined boots and hard eyes completed the picture of well-disciplined soldiers.

"Major Park Sun Yee." The Korean officer bowed sharply as he extended his hand.

"Rance Pollock," Bolan replied.

As soon as the rest of the team had been introduced, Bolan quickly briefed the new arrivals on the situation they were facing. The major didn't flinch when he heard about the nuclear warhead. Park was prepared to die in the service of his country, and a nuclear explosion would at least be a quick death.

"What do you need us to do?" was all he asked.

Using the diagram of the harbor, Katz quickly ran through the assault plan. "We can do that," Park said, then smiled. "As the SAS say, it will be a piece of cake."

McCarter grinned broadly. It was nice to meet someone who spoke the King's English and wore the old school tie. He had spotted the British SAS wings above the major's right breast pocket. Those wings weren't given out to just anyone, which meant that he had earned them the hard way.

AN HOUR LATER, Bolan, Phoenix Force and the Koreans drove to the Pusan docks. The Executioner wanted to run the Koreans through his plan on board an actual ship. Kim had located a steamer in port that was about the same size and construction as the ship the North Koreans were bringing in. It would be perfect for a combat rehearsal site.

Fortunately the ship was moored at the almost-deserted north end of the port, and it had been easy to clear the dockworkers out before they started the run-through. Bolan didn't want rubbernecks checking out the action. The fewer people who knew what was going on, the better. There was always the chance of an enemy agent working on the dock.

Since they had no way of knowing if the warhead would be rigged for command detonation or set to go off with a timer, speed was essential. Once the team was on board, it would have to locate the weapon and disarm it quickly. That meant they would have to take the gangplank leading onto the ship quickly as well.

Major Park and three of his men would board the ship, posing as the usual Korean customs authorities who greeted every arriving ship. Once they had secured the head of the gangplank, Bolan and Phoenix Force would storm on board behind them. The other two ROK soldiers would join up with the Stony Man assault team to serve as interpreters and help them search the ship.

First the commandos walked through the plan, noting any place where they might have trouble if they were strongly opposed. Then, they ran through it at full speed with more of Park's men acting the part of the North Koreans. If the ship had a normal crew, the plan was workable. If there was more opposition that they expected, however, they could call for reinforcements.

After running through the initial phase of the assault twice, Bolan called for a break. "Your men are well trained, Major," he told the Korean's leader.

Park jerked his head sharply forward in the barest sketch of a bow. "Thank you, Colonel." He smiled. "I will relate your compliments to the men."

"I think everyone knows what they are going to do, so we should go back to the air base now and finish our individual preparations. We only have a few more hours before the ship comes in, and I want everyone to be well rested and ready for it."

"We will be ready, Colonel," Park vowed. "You can count on that."

CHAPTER EIGHT

Seattle, Washington

It was cold and raining when the American Airlines Boeing 757 taxied up to the jetway at the SeaTac international terminal south of Seattle.

Schwarz looked out the window of the plane at the leaden, overcast sky. "Just what I need," he groused. "I'm not dressed for this crap."

"If I remember correctly," Lyons said, "the last time I heard, you were bitching about the heat and couldn't wait to get here because it would be cool."

"Cool's okay," Schwarz said. "But I wasn't planning on taking a cold shower."

Blancanales grinned. He too had been in the great Pacific Northwest in the spring and knew the vagaries of the weather. It might be bright and sunny tomorrow, but it sure as hell was miserable today.

The three men kept to their seats as the rest of the passengers scrambled to retrieve their luggage from the overhead storage bins and then stood waiting in the aisle. As always, Able Team had packed lightly with only one carry-on bag apiece containing a change of clothing. Their combat gear and anything else they would need on the mission would be picked up in town later.

Once the crowd had thinned out, they exited the plane and found the Stony Man courier waiting to meet them as they entered the terminal. He knew the members of Able Team on sight, and after discreetly handing a briefcase to Lyons, he faded back into the crowd. The three then went straight out to the cabstand in front of the terminal.

"I've always liked this town," Lyons said, catching the cold rain on his face as they hailed a taxi to take them into town. "It's what San Francisco should have been."

"I'd like it a hell of a lot more if it was a tad drier," Schwarz mumbled and turned up his collar. When the cab pulled up to the curb in front of them, he was the first one through the door.

On the way into Seattle, Lyons went over the contents of the briefcase he had been handed. The more he read, the grimmer he looked.

"What's the deal this time?" Schwarz asked, catching the expression on his face.

Lyons silently handed him the intelligence summary.

"Oh shit!" he said softly before passing the paper to Blancanales.

There were more problems in Seattle than just a little nasty weather.

HAL BROGNOLA HAD PREPARED the way for them, and Le Van Pham of the DEA's Asian Gang Task Force was waiting to meet them at the Federal Building when they arrived. After the introductions had been made, with Able Team using aliases, the agent led them into the briefing room and directly over to the coffeepot.

"Okay, gentlemen," Pham said after everyone had a cup of coffee, "we have orders from the Justice Department to give you our fullest cooperation, so how can I help you?"

"The first thing we need," Carl Lyons, a.k.a. Jerry Simpson, said, "is an update on Korean gang activity over the past couple of weeks. And not just here in Seattle. All up and down the coast."

"That's easy," Pham replied. "I can answer that in one word—nothing."

"What do you mean?"

"There's been a radical downturn in Korean gang activity over the past several weeks. They even called a cease-fire with their traditional enemies, the Vietnamese gangs and the Chinese tongs."

"Do you know why?"

Pham shook his head. "Not really. We're working on the premise that they're going in together on some kind of major operation. But so far we don't have a clue as to what it will be."

"We might be able to shed a little light on that," Lyons said grimly.

After reading the federal agent the *Official Secrets Act,* Lyons quickly briefed him on the missing Russian warheads, the possible Chinese or North Korean connection and the threat of nuclear terrorism in the Pacific Rim.

Pham paled. "You're joking!"

One look at the expression on Lyons's face told him the gravity of the situation.

"But how does that tie in with a street-gang cease-fire. I don't understand. Since when did gangs get into the nuke weapons business? That's terrorist stuff."

Lyons went on to tell Pham the theory of the warheads being used for nuclear blackmail in the Pacific Rim and of their being transported to their targets on commercial shipping.

"If that's true," Pham said thoughtfully, "we've got a real problem here. As you know, Seattle is a major Pacific Rim import hub, and we get a lot of Red Chinese shipping that stops in North Korea before coming here. Any one of those ships could have one of those bombs on board!"

"You've got the picture," Blancanales said. "And we're not only talking about Seattle. Anyplace from Vancouver, B.C., to San Diego could be a target.''

''Oh shit.''

For the next two hours, Pham briefed Able Team on the West Coast Asian gang situation. Mostly Lyons had him concentrate on the gangs running the dockside extortion operations, but he also had him go over even the minor gangs, the pimps and the drug pushers, as well.

''How about getting an intel summary printout on all of these organizations?'' Lyons asked when he was finished.

''They're available,'' Pham said. ''I'll have the printouts made.''

''Okay. Also, how about a list of the local hangouts and gang members? As long as we're here, we might as well see what we can find out.''

''That'll take a little while to put together,'' the DEA man said. ''But I can have it for you first thing in the morning.''

''In the meantime,'' Lyons told him, ''I'd like you to get your people out on the streets and see if there's any rumors about something 'special' going down. Concentrate your efforts here in Seattle, San Francisco, Los Angeles and San Diego first.''

''I can get the task force going on that immediately,'' Pham said. ''Since the cease-fire, things have been pretty quiet lately and we haven't had that much to do."

"Just remember that you can't tell any of your agents about the missing warheads. The President has ordered that aspect of the operation be kept strictly secret. Even though there's no evidence that any of the missing warheads are targeted against us, he's afraid of a nationwide panic if any of this gets out."

"I can certainly understand that," Pham replied.

As soon as the intel summary printouts were ready, Lyons stuffed them in his briefcase. "This will do for now," he told the agent. "I want to get us checked into our rooms and start going over this material. We'll plan to hit the streets tomorrow morning and see what we can turn up here. If I have any questions, I'll give you a call."

"If I'm not here, you can ask for Jim Pao, my second in command."

"Catch you in the morning."

AFTER THE MEETING broke up, Pham went back to his office and sent the orders out to all the branch offices of the Asian Gang Task Force. When that was done, he quickly changed into his street clothes. Even though he had all of his people out hitting every contact they had, he knew how long it could take to develop a lead. In a situation this important, time was critical, and he was afraid that it wasn't going to happen fast enough.

Simpson hadn't said anything about Seattle being any more of a potential target than any other West Coast port city. But, because of the amount of Red Chinese shipping that came in, it had to be in the top three. He had a couple of personal contacts that only he could talk to, and to do that, he had to hit the bricks himself.

As soon as he was dressed, he checked the load in the magazine of his 10 mm Glock pistol and holstered it under his left arm inside his windbreaker. The jacket was loose enough that the weapon wouldn't show if he kept the zipper caught at the bottom. He usually went unarmed on the streets, but if things were as serious as Simpson had said, he wanted the added assurance of the powerful pistol. He didn't clip his personal communicator to the front of his belt, however. Where he was going today, it would be a dead giveaway that he was a cop.

"I'm going to be out of contact for a few hours," he told the agent in the outer office. "I'll be back at about four or five."

"Right, sir. If anyone calls, where do you want me to say that you've gone?"

"I'm going to visit some of my relatives."

"Yes, sir."

The Federal Building was only a few blocks from the part of the city that was starting to be called "Little Saigon North." In the late seventies and early eighties, it had been a chic, upscale area full of overpriced tourist-trap antique shops and boutiques known as Pioneer Square. By the late eighties, however, economic realities had prevailed and the area quickly slid downhill, becoming a haven for drug users and prostitutes as soon the sun went down.

With the fall in real-estate prices, Asian immigrants had started buying into the area, replacing the pricey antique shops with small Asian stores, Oriental restaurants and tea shops. They had been so successful at their enterprises that the Asian population had spread through much of the older part of town from the harbor to the Kingdome stadium.

The first block presented a colorful Oriental facade, and was relatively accessible to the public. Several blocks into Little Saigon North, however, was a warren of small stalls and tables on the sidewalk that resembled the back alleys of any crowded Asian city. Quite a few of Pham's relatives lived in the area, and he spent many hours there. But, like today, most of his visits were strictly business.

Sitting down at a sidewalk table in front of a tiny Vietnamese soup shop, he lighted up a cigarette. Pham normally didn't smoke, but the cigarette was

camouflage, as were the black pants and white shirt
he wore with the gaudy windbreaker. To an out-
sider, he would look like any of a dozen other
Asians passing time at one of the dozen similar small
establishments that lined the block.

The waiter, an older man, quickly approached.
"Chao ong," he greeted Pham politely.

"Chao ong, Ba Moui Ba," he answered, then ordered the French beer once very popular with the
millions of American GIs in Southeast Asia.

The waiter quickly returned and glanced up and
down the street as he placed a glass in front of the
cop and poured the beer. "It is dangerous for you to
be seen here," he told Pham.

Pham slowly took a drink. "And why is that?"

"They know who you are," the old man answered. "And they have been talking about you and
your men." The waiter didn't have to explain who
"they" were. Pham knew that the man referred to
the Black Fist, Seattle's biggest Vietnamese gang,
run by the infamous Tran Van Deng.

Deng had been a corrupt South Vietnamese official who had escaped the country when Saigon fell
in 1975. Making a new start in Los Angeles, he had
built up a sizable criminal enterprise based on gambling, loan-sharking and drug dealing. When he
became wealthy enough, he moved his headquarters to Seattle, where he had added dockside extor-

tion to his operation. He was reported to be doing very well at it, particularly with the shipments from Asia. If there was anything coming in on a ship from China, Deng would be the one to know about it.

"They are showing pictures of you to the cowboys," the waiter continued. "And they are offering a big reward if you have an 'accident.'"

"Cowboy" was the Vietnamese nickname for the petty gangsters that plagued every Asian refugee community. Usually younger than the full-fledged gang members, the cowboys served as runners and auxiliaries for the Black Fist. If they did well with their youthful violent assignments, they would be rewarded by being accepted into the ranks of the gangs as full-fledged members.

"They have known who I am for a long time," Pham replied. "Why do they want me dead now?"

"I do not know."

"What else are you hearing?" the agent asked.

The old man paused. "Something important is happening," he said slowly, "but they fall silent when I bring them their drinks, so I hear nothing." He thought for a moment. "Also, I see many of the young men drinking with the Chinese and Korean tong people."

That confirmed the truce that had been reported. Usually the only time the Vietnamese, Chinese and Korean gangs got together was to kill one another.

"What else have you seen them doing together?"

"After they drink, they walk back together to a building in the next block on King Street. The big brick building with the photo shop on the corner."

Pham knew the place. "What's in that building?"

"Only one of Deng's gambling parlors on the top floor."

The agent thought for a moment. Deng had never been known to open one of his establishments to his traditional enemies, so something was going down other than crooked high-stakes gambling. Something that he would like to know about. Maybe this was the place to look for the lead he needed.

He drained the last of his beer and slid his chair back. Laying a folded bill under his glass, he got to his feet. "Goodbye," he said to the waiter.

The waiter bowed slightly and slid his hand over the bill.

Pham lighted another cigarette and walked around the corner to the street the gambling hall was on. He knew he was taking a big risk going in there alone, but he was anxious to get a lead on this thing and was counting on Deng's men not expecting a

federal drug agent to walk into one of his strong-
holds. Maybe he'd even stop off at one of the tables
and play a few hands of cards. Maybe he'd even get
lucky and win back the fifty dollars he had paid the
old man for his information.

CHAPTER NINE

Pusan, Korea

Mack Bolan and Phoenix Force waited inside the shadows of a deserted warehouse at the end of the Pusan harbor. On the other side of the dock, Major Park and his special forces team started up the gangplank of the North Korean vessel. Posing as custom inspectors, their job was to neutralize any security force that might be at the head of the gangplank and gain a foothold on the ship. Once the point of entry was secured, Phoenix Force would join them to search for the deadly cargo.

Bolan had initially thought about having himself and Phoenix Force go in as the initial assault team, but there was no way they could pass for South Koreans. Their distinctive racial characteristics dictated that Park and his men board first, and alone. The Stony Man warriors were within supporting range, and there was a heavy contingent of Korean tactical police reinforcements hiding just out of sight around the end of the dock.

But if the Korean soldiers walked into an ambush, they would be on their own for the first few critical seconds. Park understood the risk, and had willingly accepted it as necessary.

"Striker," Katz warned over the radio, "I think we've got some kind of screwup over there."

Bolan looked across the dock and saw Park arguing with three men at the head of the gangplank. One of the North Koreans looked as if he were a ship's officer, and it seemed he was trying to keep the South Koreans from boarding the ship.

"Heads up!" Bolan transmitted. "It looks like it's going down!"

A muffled shot was heard, and one of the South Koreans went down. Whipping their weapons out, Major Park and the rest of his men swept to the head of the gangplank in a storm of gunfire. The three North Koreans fell as the assault team raced up onto the deck and took cover against the ship's superstructure.

"Go! Go! Go!" Bolan called out.

The six Stony Man warriors broke from cover and raced for the end of the gangplank a hundred yards distant. Halfway across the concrete dock, a man appeared on top of the ship's bridge house with an AKM in his hands and leaned over to sight in the running men. Without breaking stride, McCarter fired a long burst from his MP-5 in his direction.

The North Korean gunman dropped down under cover, and, when he popped up again, one of Park's men drilled him through the head.

Reaching the bottom of the gangplank, the six warriors fired from the hip as they charged up the metal steps. Reaching the main deck, they leapt over the bodies and dived for cover behind the ship's superstructure. Two more bullet-riddled North Korean bodies lay on the deck, but there was no shortage of gunmen left on their feet. Apparently the ship was carrying a large crew, and it was well armed.

A burst of 7.62 mm bullets slammed into the bulkhead in front of Bolan's face. He went flat on the deck and grabbed an M-26 fragmentation grenade from his combat harness. Pulling the pin, he released the spoon and counted down three seconds. On the count of three, he tossed the bomb around the corner, where it detonated almost instantly.

The explosion was followed by a cry of pain. But, before Bolan could advance, another burst of AK fire splattered the deck in front of him.

"I've got him," Katzenelenbogen shouted as he triggered a long burst. "You're clear now."

Three North Koreans appeared at the back of the bridge deck, the AKM assault rifles in their hands switched down to full automatic. Sweeping the deck with a steady stream of 7.62 mm fire, they forced the Stony Man warriors to duck back under cover.

Caught out in the open, the Korean assault team raced for safety against the side of the bridge house. In the mad dash, one of them took a slug low in the side. He stumbled, but was jerked to safety.

"Cover me!" McCarter yelled as he slapped a fresh magazine into his MP-5. Jerking a frag grenade from his combat harness, he pulled the pin and threw the lethal egg onto the bridge deck.

When the North Koreans ducked for cover, the Briton raced across the open deck, skidding to a halt with his back against the base of the bridge. When one of the North Koreans leaned over the railing, he triggered a burst that punched the man backward. Panicked, his two companions tried to make a run for it only to be cut down by Katzenelenbogen and Bolan.

Now that they were no longer pinned down, the two teams could go to work. Under covering fire from Phoenix Force, Park and his men worked their way back to the middle of the deck, systematically clearing everything before them. At one time the ship had been a coastal transport, and it still had passenger cabins above deck. Each cabin had to be checked out before they could pass it by.

"Major Park!" McCarter yelled over the sounds of battle. "Watch your left flank!"

The Koreans turned in time to catch sight of an AK muzzle poking out from a half-opened hatch. A quick burst of gunfire followed by a frag tossed into the doorway ended that particular threat.

The major saluted McCarter before he moved out again. When the Korean assault team was halted by heavy fire from the rear of the ship, Bolan and the Briton moved up to lend a hand while the rest of the Stony Man commandos mopped up behind them.

The remainder of the North Korean crew had taken cover behind the crates lashed to the rear deck and were going to have to be dug out one at a time. Laying aside his MP-5, Bolan drew his .44 Magnum Desert Eagle. The powerful pistol could punch through the crates where the lighter 9 mm rounds might not.

Taking aim with a two-handed stance, Bolan fired at his first target, the roar of the .44 sounding clear above the noise of the firefight. When the man behind the crate panicked and broke from cover, Bolan sent a second round into his back, breaking his spine and slamming him down on his face.

Another crewman hiding in a ventilator intake made the mistake of firing at the Executioner. Rolling out of the way, Bolan snapped a return shot at the North Korean. The big .44 Magnum slug punched cleanly through the sheet metal and took the gunner in the belly. He slid to the deck clutching his gut and writhing in pain. Bolan drilled a second round into his head to put him out of his misery.

"The bow section's cleared," Katz reported over his earphone.

"So's the midsection," James added.

Though there was still scattered firing, the crew's resistance had finally been broken. Time to start the search for the stolen warhead.

"Rafael!" Bolan radioed. "You and Gary go below deck and start looking for that bomb. We'll cover you, but stay alert when you get down there."

"We're on it."

Motioning for Manning to follow him, the Cuban dashed out from cover and raced for the nearest hatchway leading down into the bowels of the ship. Snatching a frag grenade from his combat harness, he pulled the pin and tossed the bomb through the hatch to clear the way. When the explosion echoed away, he and Manning disappeared into the smoke.

Behind them, Bolan, their Phoenix Force comrades and the South Koreans mopped up the last few North Koreans. Those who surrendered were quickly taken into custody and cuffed. Those who didn't give up were dealt with summarily.

"WE'VE FOUND IT, Striker!" Encizo's voice in Bolan's earphone sounded loud after the rattle of small-arms fire. "It's in the engine room, third deck down."

"I'm on the way," the warrior answered. Calling for Calvin James to follow him, he started for the gangway leading down into the ship. Reaching the ladder, he hurried down to the third deck and took the catwalk back to the cluttered engine room at the rear of the ship.

"Over here," Encizo called out as he stepped into the open at the far end of the room.

Bolan saw Manning and the Cuban standing over a large opened shipping crate marked with Korean characters. "I picked it up with the radiac meter the minute we stepped in here," Manning said. "It looks like they took the missile's ballistic nose shielding off to save weight, and that mother's dirty without it."

James unconsciously backed away from the crate. Bullets he could handle, but he didn't like nuclear radiation one little bit.

The two-kiloton RK-36 warhead wasn't a particularly impressive-looking device. It was a thick sheet-steel sphere eighteen inches in diameter, with a small electronic control box attached to one end. Color-coded wires ran from the control box to terminals spaced evenly around the metal sphere. A small electronic timer had been attached to the control box, which displayed digital numbers counting down.

As Bolan watched, the seconds ticked off. "Can you disarm it, Gary?"

Manning dropped to one knee beside the open crate and began to examine the small device. "If what the Russians have told us is correct, it doesn't look like it's been booby-trapped," he announced. "All they did was add the timer to the firing circuit."

"Can you turn it off?"

"I don't want to mess with the timing device in case it has been fitted with some kind of antitampering circuitry. But I should be able to separate the warhead from the firing circuit itself so that it can't detonate."

"Do it," Bolan ordered.

Reaching into the pouch strapped to his hip, the Canadian pulled out a circuit tester and a pair of insulated wire cutters. Ever so carefully, he started testing the electrical circuits. Stopping every now and then to check his schematic diagram of the warhead's detonation system, he quickly traced down the weapon's primary firing circuit.

When he had assured himself that the North Koreans hadn't added a booby-trap circuit to the device, he snipped a pair of wires and folded them back out of the way. Taking a screwdriver from his pouch, he cautiously removed the eight screws holding the cover of the control box in place. Removing the cover, he reached in with the wire cutters again and snipped the main lead to the microswitch sequencer. Four more screws and the sequencer was free.

"There," Manning said as he stood, the sequencer in his hand. "It's as safe as I can make it down here. We have to do the rest back at the air base."

WHEN THE MESSAGE had been sent that the warhead was secured and ready to go, a small convoy of three South Korean V-100 Commando armored cars and a van roared onto the dock, screeching to a halt in front of the ship. A pair of camouflage-painted ROK army AH-1S Cobra helicopter gunships roared through the sky and banked to circle low over the dock area. The 20 mm Vulcan cannon in their nose turrets swiveled from side to side, ready to open up at the slightest sign of trouble.

The five men from the American NOD team jumped out of the van carrying what looked like a stretcher with web straps to tie down a patient. Rushing up the ship's gangplank, they were directed to the rear deck where Manning and James had brought the nuke up from the hold.

When the NOD team came back down the gang-plank with the warhead on their stretcher, they walked slowly, watching where they put their feet with each step. The warhead had been disarmed, but it still contained several pounds of high explosives with sensitive detonators attached and was still dangerous.

Once on the dock, the warhead was carefully loaded into the van, tied down, and the rear doors locked behind it. Sirens wailing, the small convoy pulled away from the dock area and headed back to the American Air Force base at the edge of town.

The two ROK army gunships banked away from the harbor to follow the convoy.

CHAPTER TEN

Pusan AFB

At the U.S. air base, the team of nuclear weapons disposal experts from both the United States and Russia carefully went to work on the warhead to render it completely safe.

The weapon was a subcritical-mass implosion-type design. Therefore, without the microswitch sequencer that Gary Manning had removed, it couldn't go into nuclear detonation. However, the shaped explosive blocks that created the implosion necessary to initiate the nuclear detonation were still around the hollow mass of the plutonium core. If one of them exploded, even though the warhead wouldn't go nuclear, it would scatter the highly radioactive and toxic plutonium over a wide area.

First, the spherical steel housing was removed from the warhead, revealing the machined explosive blocks surrounding the nuclear core. By themselves, the blocks were only precisely shaped, ultrafast-detonating plastic explosive and were no more dangerous than any other high explosive. But when detonated in the proper sequence, they created an explosive wave that imploded the subcritical mass of plutonium and forced it into a shape that would create, and sustain, a nuclear reaction.

Carefully, and in sequence, the detonators were removed from the explosive blocks one at a time. When they had all been taken away, the machined explosive blocks themselves were carefully separated from the nuclear material.

When the last of the explosive blocks had been removed, the warhead was finally harmless—if a ten-kilo mass of weapons-grade plutonium could ever be considered safe. The nuclear material itself would be returned to Russian control for conversion into peaceful nuclear-reactor fuel.

When the NOD team declared the warhead safe, Bolan immediately headed for the base communications center to make his report.

"ONE DOWN," Aaron Kurtzman stated when Bolan told him that the warhead had been captured and rendered harmless, "and only nine to go. All we have to do now is find the rest of them."

"We'll find them," the Executioner replied, his voice grim over the secure line. "One way or the other, Bear, we'll find them."

"I know that. But will we be in time?"

"We have no choice. If we don't, this whole region will go up in a mushroom cloud. Do you have anything on them yet?"

"Not yet, but we have everyone from Moscow to Tokyo working on it. We're bound to come up with something before too long."

"Make it sooner rather than later, Bear."

As soon as Bolan hung up, Kurtzman wheeled his chair around to face Gregori Klimov. "I guess I owe you an apology."

Though the discovery of the warhead on the North Korean ship had vindicated his theory, the Russian had the good graces and the common sense not to gloat about it.

"That's not important," the Russian answered. "We are all in this together. The important thing is that we still do not know where the rest of the warheads are being held. Finding them one by one is all fine and good. Just as long, that is, as we can find them in time. But if we can locate where they are being held, we can end this once and for all."

Barbara Price walked over to a large map of the Pacific Ocean projected on the big wall screen and studied it for a moment. "I think it's safe to assume—" she glanced over at Klimov "—that the rest of the warheads are in the Far East as you predicted they would be, and that they are targeted against the Pacific Rim nations. That means that we can stand down the search teams working the Middle East and Europe and can concentrate all our efforts in this area."

"It might be a good idea," Klimov suggested, "to inform the SEATO nations of this incident and have them keep a close eye on any North Korean vessels scheduled to enter their waters."

"And aircraft," Jack Grimaldi, the Stony Man pilot, added. "Even though the North Koreans don't fly to many other nations, other people's airliners land at Pyongyang before going on to somewhere else. It'd be all too easy to slip a nuke on board without anyone being the wiser."

"That's a good point," Kurtzman replied.

"I'll call Hal," Price said. "He'll want to know about this."

DENG'S BUILDING in Seattle took up most of the block. It was a large turn-of-the-century three-story brick structure that had been converted into shops and apartments. The ground floor housed an Oriental restaurant, a camera shop, a garage and a small Asian grocery store, all legitimate businesses that were owned by Deng.

A stairwell at the end of the building led up to the apartments on the second floor, which were legitimate, too, a screen for the gambling den on the third floor. Officially the third floor was a legal but private Vietnamese social club. The DEA knew about Deng's gambling operation, but since there had been no reports of drug dealing on the premises they had left it alone. The Feds didn't care about illegal card games. The Seattle police department apparently wasn't concerned, either, because Deng had been operating the business for several years.

The door at the top of the stairs that led onto the second floor wasn't locked, and Pham went right in. As he walked down the long hall between the apartments, the pungent odors of Oriental cooking wafted through the air. They brought Pham cherished memories of a childhood spent in a building in California very much like this one.

At the end of the corridor, a modern steel fire door closed off another stairwell leading to the top floor. From the weight of the door when he opened it, Pham knew that it was armored. Without being too obvious about it, he noted the massive remote-controlled electronic lock, the same kind that was used to lock jail cell doors.

He looked for a video-camera head, but didn't see one. That didn't mean that the door wasn't under observation, however. Miniature video cameras not much larger than a pencil eraser could be hidden anywhere along the hall. It was possible that he was walking into a trap that could be snapped shut behind him at any moment, and he felt a tingle run down his spine.

Pham almost turned around and left. He knew that he was getting in well over his head. He should simply take what he had learned and report back to Simpson, but he continued up the stairs. He had come this far and didn't want to waste the effort.

At the top of the stairs was a bright red, ornately carved wooden door. At least it looked like it was wood. It could have been molded bulletproof Lexan plastic for all he knew. The sign, in Vietnamese, read Triple Happiness Social Club. The first "Happiness" was obviously gambling, and he wondered what other two vices would generate happiness. A buzzer was set into the wall under the sign, and he pressed the button.

As before, he couldn't see any video-camera heads, but again he had a tingling sensation that he was being watched. The red door unlocked with a buzz and opened a few inches. He pushed it the rest of the way open and walked into a dimly lighted, short hallway. Before Pham's eyes could adjust to the light, he heard the door click shut and lock behind him and knew that he had stepped into deep trouble.

A guard with a MAC-10 submachine gun sat at a small table, and the muzzle was aimed squarely at Pham's chest. The man standing beside the guard was Le Duc Minh, Deng's second in command, and Minh knew the DEA agent well. They had grown up on the same crowded streets of the Vietnamese quarter of L.A. together. Pham had heard that Minh had come to Seattle to work for Deng, but this was the first time he had seen him since the good old days.

Minh smiled slowly as he drew an automatic pistol from under his suit jacket. "Raise your hands carefully."

Pham did exactly as he had been told. The guard frisked him, discovered the Glock pistol in the shoulder holster and relieved him of it.

"Turn around and put your hands behind your back," Minh commanded.

Again Pham didn't resist as the guard quickly slipped a plastic restraint over the cop's wrists, snugged it down tight and turned him around again.

"It has been a long time since we have seen each other, Le Van Pham," Minh said, "but it was very foolish for you to have come here."

Pham had no choice but to agree.

Minh led Pham around the corner of the hall to an elevator. Taking a magnetically coded security card from his pocket, he unlocked the door and motioned the agent inside. Shielding the control panel from Pham's view, Minh slipped his card into a slot and pushed a button. The elevator silently started down.

When Minh moved out of the way, Pham could see that there were no numbers on the buttons of the control panel, but there were four buttons. Since there were only three floors aboveground, the other button had to be for an unseen basement floor. From the time that the elevator took to make its descent, Pham figured that they had gone all the way to the bottom floor.

The door opened to a brightly lighted, modern office full of Asians. Attractive girls in colorful silk *ao dais,* the Vietnamese national dress, sat behind computer keyboards and answered phones. Others were packing files into cardboard boxes and running papers through a shredder. No one was in a panic, but everyone was working as quickly as they could. It was obvious that Deng was moving his operation out of there as fast as he could.

Pham was taken through the office to a door at the far end of the room. Minh knocked lightly and a voice speaking Vietnamese ordered them to enter. The guard immediately opened the door and shoved Pham into a lavishly furnished room. The walls were covered with carved wooden panels and ancient Chinese art prints. The floor was carpeted with priceless Oriental rugs that would have cost Pham at least a year's salary. The man sitting behind the ornately carved wooden desk at the end of the room was thin with a sharp face, a face that Pham knew well from his files.

"Tran Van Deng, I presume," he said in English.

Deng studied him for a moment, his deep-set eyes seeming to burn into him. "You have made a grave mistake by coming here, Le Van Pham of the DEA's Asian Gang Task Force," he answered in Vietnamese.

"I just wanted to play a couple hands of cards upstairs," he said with a big smile, trying to brazen it out.

Deng stared at him for a long moment. "I do not think it is that simple," he finally said. "You are poking your nose into something that is none of your business."

Pham just shrugged his shoulders. There was no point in playing dumb. Deng was the leader of a vicious criminal gang, and he wasn't stupid. He obviously was afraid that the authorities were on to him for something or he wouldn't be preparing to abandon his comfortable headquarters.

"What do you want me to do with him?" Minh asked his leader.

Deng thought for a moment. If he killed this federal cop, it might cause him a little more trouble than he had time to deal with right now. He knew how the DEA reacted when one of their officers was murdered. Right now, the schedule for the operation didn't include any time to waste hiding from vengeful Feds.

He also couldn't afford to just turn Pham loose, even though he would be cleared out of the building by the day after tomorrow. He didn't know how much the cop had learned. Maybe it would be best if Pham just disappeared for a while. He could have one of his men wear Pham's clothing and use his DEA identification and make sure he was seen around town. That should divert the DEA long enough for him to put the plan into operation.

Deng looked at the DEA man for a long moment. "Lock him up and we will take him with us when we go."

The guard took Pham's arm. "Where are you taking me?"

"I'm just making sure you keep out of my way for a while," Deng said. "You will be released later."

Though he wanted to believe Deng, Pham knew that he wouldn't be freed later. Even though he didn't know why it was being done, simply knowing that Deng was moving his base of operations meant that he knew too much. The only way he was going to get out of this was if Jerry Simpson and his friends got into the act. And he knew that they would come for him. They also thought that he knew too much.

CHAPTER ELEVEN

Pyongyang, North Korea

The North Korean capital city of Pyongyang wasn't at all like the cities of South Korea. Seoul, Pusan and Tagu in the South all showed the signs of capitalistic growth run wild. Newly constructed buildings and homes sprawled out over the countryside with more construction getting underway every day. Though it was as new as any of the southern cities, there was none of this growth in Pyongyang.

The northern capital was a static, sterile, overly planned monolithic monument to communism, existing solely to house and serve the Communist government. One of the government agencies the city served was the dreaded Liaison Bureau, the North Korean equivalent of the old Soviet KGB. And while the KGB was dead in Mother Russia, the Liaison Bureau was very much alive in North Korea.

In a small branch office of the Liaison Bureau in the outskirts of the city, Major Lim Son Rae's hands shook with rage.

"We were betrayed." The Liaison Bureau officer's voice was hard as he read the transcript he had just been handed by one of his communications-room runners. "There is no other way the South Koreans could have known that the warhead was hidden on that ship."

Though he was relatively junior in rank, Lim led a clique of senior North Korean officers and Korean Communist Party officials who were concerned about the direction their nation was headed. The father of Communist North Korea, Kim Il Sung, was old and the dictator's powers were swiftly fading. There were even those of his closest circle who said that he was becoming more senile and incontinent every day.

The fear wasn't that the Iron Man of the North would soon die—everyone had to die. The fear was what would become of North Korea upon his death. Kim's son and heir apparent was a weak man, a worthless Western-influenced playboy and a disgrace to his father's name.

The younger Kim had gathered a group of advisers around him who expected to rule North Korea as soon as the elder Kim went to his ancestors. The younger Kim wasn't that young himself—he was in his sixties—and he had waited a long time to claim his inheritance. But his idea of the good life did not include living a disciplined Marxist existence. From all the information that Lim had been able to collect about the younger Kim and his circle of intimate advisers, they intended to turn North Korea into a pale imitation of the decadent, capitalistic South.

Major Lim Son Rae was the descendant of people who had been peasants for over a thousand years, and he looked it. He had the round-moon flat face and stocky body of Korean peasant stock. He was strong as a man can only be after centuries of harsh genetic selection. His genetic stock was strong because the weak quickly died in his harsh country.

His relative low rank, however, was a reflection of how far out of favor the hard-line Korean Marxists had become recently. He should have been promoted to lieutenant-colonel long ago, but he had spoken out strongly against the trend of relaxing the standards that had made North Korea a Pacific power to be feared. Even though his hard-line Marxist views had kept him from his rightful position in the current government's hierarchy, Lim would rather die before he would even consider changing his beliefs.

Lim was proud of his peasant heritage, but everything he was today he owed to the Communist Party of North Korea. The fact that he could read and do mathematics was only because of the Communist school he had attended. His having been chosen to become an officer cadet had been solely because of his devotion to the ideals of communism. Only in a true worker's society could a man of such humble beginnings as himself have gone from the manure pile of his family's small farm to a position of power in the Korean government. As a result of that, his life was dedicated to ensuring that the system that had given him so much was never changed.

"This is but a minor setback, Comrade Lim," the Vietnamese intelligence officer standing next to him said soothingly. "Our plan is sound, and it cannot fail. Thanks to the Russians, we have nine more warheads and we need only to detonate one or two of them for us to achieve our goals."

Allied with Lim's Marxist group was a cadre of hard-core Marxist Vietnamese led by another junior officer, Major Nguyen Le Thant. The Vietnamese conspirators were also concerned about their government's plan to open their socialist nation to capitalistic ventures. Their freedom from capitalism had been hard-won and had cost well over a million Vietnamese lives. They wouldn't sit by and watch those sacrifices go for nothing merely to gain a small place in the so-called world market. When the North Koreans had approached them with a plan for a New Revolution, they had eagerly joined forces.

Thant was of an old family of imperial aristocrats, and the main problem he had experienced working with the North Korean was Lim's volatility. Since infancy, Thant had been taught to expect the unexpected and to always have patience. The more intense Lim, however, lacked the virtue of patience and demanded instant solutions to problems that had been years in the making.

Thant had learned about patience during his nation's long war for independence against first the Japanese during World War II, then the French and later the Americans. Even the invincible Americans with their endless weapons had been driven out of his country more by the application of patience than by force.

When General Vo Nguyen Giap had tried to destroy the Americans during the Tet Offensive of 1968, the Yankees had inflicted a severe blow to the North Vietnamese army. The defeat had been so serious that it had taken years to fully recover from it. The final victory over the South in 1975 had only been achieved by patiently waiting for the Americans to tire of the war and abandon their onetime allies to their fate.

Patience was essential this time, too, if the New Revolution was to be successful. And successful it would be. When this operation was concluded, it would be Vietnam and North Korea who would be the emerging political powers of the Pacific Rim, not China. China would be in a shambles, an Asian Yugoslavia trying to recover from the punishment they were sure to receive from the Western nations.

"Nonetheless," Lim hissed, "we were betrayed. We must tighten security, and I will track down those who sold us out to the imperialists."

"Is that wise, comrade?" the Vietnamese questioned. "Might that not bring unwanted attention to our activities? We have escaped notice so far, and it must stay that way until we are ready to strike."

"You have a point, Comrade," Lim admitted. "And that is why we have to be even more careful about security now that the operation is finally under way."

"The next target is Singapore, correct?" Thant asked, trying to keep the conversation to the subject.

The Vietnamese knew full well what the next target was, just as he knew all of the other eight if it was necessary to carry their operation that far. But he wanted to get the Korean focused on the matter at hand. It was important that the first warhead be detonated as soon as possible so the New Revolution could go ahead as planned.

He knew that it might take only one warhead to bring the downfall of the Chinese. No matter where the warhead was detonated, the Western powers would have to act quickly to prevent further nuclear devastation. They would blame the Chinese for the incident and demand that they disarm themselves under UN supervision or face immediate war.

The mere threat of renewed war with the West had worked with Saddam Hussein and Iraq after the Gulf War, but it wouldn't work with the Chinese. There was no way that the proud Chinese would stand aside and allow Western inspection teams to watch while they destroyed their nuclear arsenal. Particularly when they knew full well that they had had nothing at all to do with the incident.

They would rightfully claim innocence. But the Westerners would equally claim that their scientific instruments had identified the weapon as having been Chinese. The Americans had a satellite-borne nuclear-event-detection system code-named Forest Green that would make videotapes of the detonation. The satellite's instruments would also record the weapon's distinctive nuclear signature, which would positively identify it as being Chinese.

"Yes," Lim said, walking over to the map of the Pacific Rim mounted on the wall of his office, "Singapore is next. The warhead is being loaded on board the Chinese ship in Cam Ranh Bay right now."

Part of the deception plan was that, except for the first warhead, the rest would be carried to their final destinations on board Chinese-registered vessels.

Working with the Vietnamese and North Korean Marxists was a small number of younger, hard-line Maoist Chinese who were also unhappy with the direction of their nation's current government. Even though the current leadership had ruthlessly put down the abortive "prodemocracy" movement in 1989, they were still racing down the golden road to capitalism as fast as they could go. Almost every month brought announcements of new trade agreements with the West.

The Chinese conspiracy wanted to see China strong and true, but they saw strength only in the teachings of Chairman Mao. They didn't want to see the return of the wealthy merchant and landowning classes that had been the downfall of Old China. They knew that Lim's New revolution would mean that their nation would be severely punished by the West, but they were willing to suffer for a few years if, at the end, China would be back on track and faithfully following the principles of Chairman Mao.

If a few thousand people had to suffer and die for those goals, it would be a small price to pay. Particularly if those who paid were the very ones who were betraying the revolution. What were the lives of a few cowardly, reactionary old men and the extermination of the greedy entrepreneurs compared to the creation of a real worker's paradise?

Nothing would remain of the ship after the detonation in Singapore except radioactive particles, but that wouldn't matter. It would be known that a Chinese ship had been in the harbor when the incident occurred. Also, the detonation was timed to go off when an American spy satellite was directly overhead. It would record the arrival of the Chinese ship on one pass overhead, and it would record the nuclear detonation the next time it came around.

There was no way that the Western powers wouldn't believe that the Chinese had been responsible for the destruction of the center of Singapore and the deaths of thousands of its inhabitants.

"But," Lim said, "that does not mean that we cannot go ahead with the other part of the operation now. The South Korean gangsters are ready to transport your heroin as soon as you can get it to us."

Thant hid a grimace. A man of fastidious personal habits, he was completely disgusted by drugs of all kinds, except of course, for nicotine and alcohol. But even them he used as sparingly as he used women. All three had their uses, but a man was a fool to give his life over to any of them.

Rampant illegal drug use was the crowning symbol of the decadent West. The fact that it was the major destroyer of their culture was the only reason he had agreed to get involved with this aspect of Lim's operation. Drugs were a powerful weapon, and any weapon was welcome in the fight to reestablish the true People's revolution. The New Revolution required a great deal of money for weapons and bribes, and Lim's smuggling operation would provide the money they needed for their cause.

Though he wasn't naive, Thant was still surprised at the number of otherwise honorable men and woman who would betray everything they held dear for mere money. This was only one more reason why he had dedicated himself to seeing that decadent capitalism never got a foothold in Vietnam. With capitalism would come drugs and the destruction that came with them.

As an officer of the Vietnamese secret service, one of Thant's responsibilities was to monitor part of the large network of Vietnamese spies operating in the United States. The first of these spies had been infiltrated when the initial wave of Boat People had emigrated to America after the fall of the criminal Saigon regime. More had been sent in the years following, and some had even been recruited from real refugees in the States.

Some of these spies were legitimate businessmen in America, some were even local politicians. More, however, were involved in criminal activities, including drug gangs. In the past, Korean and Vietnamese gangs had battled for territory and influence with the established Chinese tongs. But now that the New Revolution had established a truce between the Korean and Vietnamese gangs, their futile battles had ended and the drug operation could begin unimpeded.

The North Koreans had made inroads into the South Korean Mafia. Several North Korean undercover agents were now trusted functionaries in the South Korean underworld. For a small percentage, they would see that the drug was smuggled into the United States on ships carrying new cars to the Pacific Northwest. From there, it would be passed on to the Korean and Vietnamese gangs for street sale. The difference between this and any other drug operation would be in the volume and purity of the product.

The mountain tribes of Vietnam, those people the Americans had called the Montagnards, had been put to producing opium poppies on a full-time basis. Government labs then rendered the raw opium into high-grade heroin, and the drug was being stockpiled for sale to buy weapons. Thant had several comrades working in the heroin operation, and they had managed to sidetrack some of the drug production for the New Revolution. More than ten metric tons of ninety-eight-percent pure heroin was waiting in the secret warehouses in Cam Ranh Bay.

With that amount of the poison powder hitting the streets of America, even after everyone had taken their commission, there would still be more than enough money left over to support the New Revolution.

"I will go back to Cam Ranh Bay and start transporting the heroin," Thant said. "The first shipments will be in South Korea within the week."

"Excellent." Lim nodded. "My agents there are ready to receive the shipments. They can have them in America before the end of the month."

"That is good because we will need the money very soon. After the warhead detonates in Singapore, we will need to be ready to pay off those who will further our cause."

CHAPTER TWELVE

After getting an early breakfast at the hotel, the men of Able Team went back to the Federal Building to check in with the DEA agent.

"It looks like our man Pham took it to the streets himself last night," Blancanales said. "He told the agent that he was going out to see his relatives and he hasn't checked back yet. And he left his personal communicator on his desk."

"Damn it!" Lyons swore. "He's supposed to be running this place, not out on the streets."

Since the Vietnamese-American Fed had been briefed on the missing Russian warheads, having him running around out there could be a major security leak.

"So, where do we find his relatives?" Lyons asked.

"They're working on that now," the Puerto Rican answered. "They've got an APB out on him. According to the agent, all he meant by talking to his relatives was that he was going down into the Vietnamese district to snoop around on his own."

"Great!" Schwarz snorted. "That's just what we need this morning. The Farm's trying to keep a tight lid on this thing and we've got a real live home boy out there doing his own thing. If he screws up and gets caught, he can blow the whole deal."

"We'd better get him back here ASAP," Blancanales added.

"When we do," Lyons told him, "I'm going to see about putting him in protective custody until this thing's over. We need him for liaison and information, not out on the streets.

"Okay, guys," Lyons added, "while his office is trying to find him, the first thing we need to do is get our hardware back. Then we hit the bricks to do our own legwork."

The Able Team warriors found their weapons waiting for them with the armorer in the DEA building's basement arms room. Rather than go through the hassle of checking them on board the commercial flight, they'd had the DEA Dallas office forward them on a government courier flight.

Lyons flashed the man his Justice Department ID card. "We're here to pick up those weapons that came in from Dallas."

"Coming up," the DEA armorer said, reaching into one of his lockers and bringing out three well-worn weapons cases.

He eyed Lyons's SPAS-12 assault shotgun enviously when the big ex-cop removed the weapon from its carrying case. "That's some serious hardware," he commented. "I wish they'd let us get some of those. All we have are pump guns."

"It's a nice piece," Lyons agreed. "I could have used this back in my old LAPD days."

The armorer's eyes got even wider when he saw Blancanales unsheath a silenced Uzi.

"Who the hell are you guys, anyway?"

Lyons looked him straight in the eyes, "We're agents of the Justice Department."

The armorer just shrugged and went back to minding his own business. There were some things that he was better off not knowing about.

The first thing the team did was to break the weapons down for a thorough cleaning. In the urgency to get to Seattle, they had been packed away filthy with Texas dust and powder residue from the fight at the airfield. The cleaning supplies were on the table at the opposite end of the room, and it took almost half an hour before the last of the Texas dust was gone and the weapons had been reassembled.

Lyons then presented the armorer with an ammunition supply request. "You guys planning on starting a war around here?" the man asked when he saw the amount of ammunition on the form.

Schwarz grinned. "Nope. We don't start wars, we finish them."

"You've got enough ammo there to start and finish a couple."

Lyons looked up. "Ammunition's like money—you can never have too much of it."

The armorer shook his head. "I'll give it to you, but you're going to have to account for that stuff, you know. That's the regulation."

"If you check in with the Department of Justice," Lyons replied, "I think you'll find that we're authorized to burn up as much as we want, no questions asked."

The armorer just shook his head.

ONCE THEY HAD SECURED their weapons and ammunition, Able Team went to the DEA intelligence office to get the printout they had ordered of the city's most prominent Vietnamese gang hangouts and front operations. Pham still hadn't checked in, and no one had been able to locate him.

"We have everyone out looking for him, sir," the senior agent said. "How will we be able to get hold of you if we find him?"

"Just find him," Lyons replied. "Hold him, and we'll get in contact with you when we can. Right now we've got work to do."

"Okay, we've got the list," Scwarz said once they were back out in the hall. "Now what do we do?"

There was no question that they had to get Pham back ASAP. If he let anything slip about his mission, mass panic would ensue. The question was, how were they going to find him in an unfamiliar city of some four million people?

"I'd say the most effective thing we can do is just get out there and rattle some cages," Blancanales suggested. "See what we turn up."

"The old Able Team 'kick ass and take names' routine." Schwarz grinned broadly. "It's crude, but effective."

"Let's do it," Lyons ordered.

Blancanales jerked his thumb back toward the DEA offices. "Do we want to let these guys know what's going down?"

"No." The big ex-cop shook his head. "They'll find out about it soon enough."

Down in the basement motor pool, Schwarz opened the trunk of the four-door sedan they had been assigned and stowed their B bags and their weapons inside. Even with the highest authority backing them up, it wouldn't do to be seen driving around the streets with submachine guns in their hands. It would make the local police understandably nervous. And since the Seattle police department hadn't been cleared to know about the missing warheads, briefing them on what they were doing was out of the question.

Considering the way Able Team operated, there was no doubt that the urban commandos would come to the attention of the local authorities sooner or later. But Hal Brognola could handle the situation when it happened. Right now, the Stony Man warriors had to go to work.

THE FIRST STOP on their list was one of Deng's smaller back-room gambling parlors in a small Vietnamese soup shop and café. Parking their car in front of the establishment, Schwarz stayed behind the wheel while Lyons and Blancanales went in. If there was any trouble, he could provide backup in seconds.

Inside the soup shop, about half a dozen tables covered with red-and-white-checked tablecloths filled most of the small room. Plastic flowers and posters and calendars were the only decoration. Ashtrays and bottles of *nouc-mam,* the fiery fermented fish sauce that was the cornerstone of Vietnamese cuisine, sat on every table.

The place was empty except for an old man sitting behind the cash register and two young Vietnamese cowboys seated at a table at the far end of the room. The gangsters were guarding the beaded curtain that closed off the dark hallway that led to the gambling room in the back, and they weren't being subtle about it. They looked up from their drinks and glared when they saw the two new arrivals enter the shop.

Lyons and Blancanales ignored the two cowboys and identified themselves to the old man as federal agents, showing him the ID cards the courier had provided in their mission packet.

"Have you seen this man lately?" Lyons asked, holding up a photo of Pham.

"I see him sometimes," the old man answered in heavily accented English. "But I no see him this week."

"When was the last time you saw him?"

"I no remember."

"You sure?"

The man nodded.

Realizing that he was getting nowhere, Lyons tried a different tack. "We also need to know where we can find a man named Tran Van Deng."

The old man's eyes narrowed when he heard Deng's name, and he nervously glanced back at the two cowboys. "I no hear of him before."

"Are you sure?"

"I very sure." The man nodded slowly. "I never hear of this man."

With the mention of Deng's name, the two cowboys in the back started talking softly. Among

Blancanales's many talents was a gift for languages. Though it had been a long time since he had been completely conversant in Vietnamese, he still had a good grasp of the language.

"The skinny guy on the left thinks that if we ever do find Deng," he whispered to Lyons, "we'll wish that we had kept our long, ugly Caucasian noses out of his business."

"Does he now?" Lyons said softly, shooting a quick glance to the back of the room.

"He also says that old men like us shouldn't be out on the streets without our nurses. We might get hurt."

"Maybe we can ask them about Deng."

"Good idea."

Lyons turned and faced the table, clearing his gun arm and his field of fire. "Do either of you speak English?"

The two Vietnamese slowly slid their chairs back and stood. "I speak English," the one on the left said. "What do you want?"

While he spoke, the other cowboy went for a weapon under his jacket. Lyons's .357 Magnum Colt Python cleared leather while the Vietnamese was still pulling his iron. Even so, the guy went for it anyway. Lyons waited until the last possible moment before the Colt roared.

The heavy slug hit the cowboy high on the left side of his chest, right over his heart. The round exploded the organ and tore through the back of his rib cage, blowing a large exit hole in his back. He was dead before he hit the floor.

The other Vietnamese hardman made a run for it, but the Beretta in Blancanales's hand spit twice, cutting the guy down in midstride. He crashed to the floor, screaming in pain.

Throughout all of this, the old man behind the cash register hadn't moved an inch. He was a veteran of the South Vietnamese army, and he had been around gunfire before. He had also seen enough combat to know that if he made any sudden move, the muzzle of the big Colt would be looking at him next.

And he had no reason to try to protect the infamous Deng. In fact, he would be more than glad to see these long noses send the gangster to his ancestors. It was difficult enough for him to make a living for his family without having to pay "taxes" to the likes of him. Also, if Deng was gone, he could expand his small café into the back room and make even more money.

Schwarz stormed through the door a second later, his H&K subgun at the ready.

"It's all over." Lyons motioned for him to put his weapon away. "Call for an ambulance and have the DEA come get the guy who's still alive."

Blancanales kneeled beside the wounded man. "Where can we find this Deng you were talking about?" he asked in fluent Vietnamese. "We want to stick our long noses in his business."

Grimacing through his pain, the gangster tried to spit at Blancanales, but it ran down his own chin instead.

"I asked you a question, friend," the Puerto Rican snapped in English, grabbing a handful of the man's shirt and jerking him up to a sitting position. "Where's Deng?"

The Vietnamese gasped with pain. "My legs!"

"Answer me, or you'll be worrying about more than your legs."

A moment later, both the ambulance and the police arrived, sirens wailing. Lyons and Schwarz went out to the sidewalk to meet them, leaving Blancanales to continue questioning the man inside. They both had their weapons holstered and their Federal ID cards out, waiting to give it to the police lieutenant who stepped out of the lead car.

"What happened in there?" the cop snapped, looking up from the ID cards.

"We were questioning the shop owner about a missing federal agent," Lyons replied, "when two punks in there went for their guns. One of them is dead, and the other's wounded.''

The cop turned to his sergeant. "Take their weapons until I get this sorted out."

"Before you get too carried away and do something like arrest us, Lieutenant," Lyons said, handing him another card, "I strongly suggest that you call this number first."

The cop glared at him, but walked over to his car and picked up the radio mike. In a moment, he was patched in to the number and was speaking with someone in the Justice Department in Washington.

While the lieutenant was on the phone, the paramedics quickly patched up the wounded man and loaded him into the ambulance. It drove away, sirens wailing.

"You get anything?" Lyons asked when Blancanales joined them on the sidewalk.

The Puerto Rican shook his head. "He was a hard case, and I didn't have enough time to work on him before the medics arrived."

"We'll just have to try again then."

CHAPTER THIRTEEN

"I don't know who in the hell you three guys are," the Seattle cop growled, eyeing Lyons coldly when he came back from making his call to check them out, "but I've been told to leave you the hell alone."

"That suits us," Lyons answered, keeping his voice neutral. "We have a job to do, and we need to get back to doing it."

"Their story checks out, Lieutenant," a Vietnamese-speaking Seattle PD cop reported after talking to the old man behind the cash register. "The guy inside says that those two cowboys started it, and these guys only fired back to protect themselves."

This wasn't what the lieutenant had wanted to hear. When he had arrived on the scene a few minutes earlier he had found one dead Vietnamese cowboy, one more wounded and these three hard cases packing enough illegal hardware to start a small war. Their ID cards claiming that they were some kind of special agents for the Department of Justice had checked out, but that didn't cut shit with him. This was his town, not L.A., and he wasn't going to have anyone shooting up the streets, Feds or not.

He was used to going head-to-head with the various federal agencies over jurisdiction issues and sometimes he even won. But the word had come down through the chief's office that these three particular Feds were to be left completely alone. All the Seattle police department was authorized to do was to clean up after them. And the chief had added that anyone on the force who couldn't go along with that program could go on an extended, unpaid leave of absence until it was over. Even so, he couldn't let it go.

"I want to advise you though," the lieutenant said, narrowing his gaze, "that you people had better keep a lid on it as long as you're in my town. I don't want any more fucking firefights in this burg."

Lyons gave him a long hard look. "That's going to depend entirely on the people that we have to talk to, Lieutenant. We didn't start this pissing contest, but we finished it. And I can assure you that if anyone else in your town decides he feels like taking a shot at us, we'll finish that fight, as well."

The Seattle cop answered Lyons's hard look with one of his own, but he knew that there wasn't a damned thing he could do about these guys.

"Just try to keep a lid on it, mister!"

Lyons gave him the last word and didn't answer. He had been a cop long enough to know where the lieutenant was coming from. No one wanted a war going on in his own backyard, not even when it was a war that had been sanctioned by the United States government.

TRAN VAN DENG looked up from his desk when his lieutenant, Minh, entered his office.

"I just got a call from Tuan, one of our runners," the Vietnamese gangster said. "It looks like we have a serious problem. Three long-nose cops are busting up our gambling joints, and they're coming in shooting."

Deng couldn't believe what he was hearing. The police in Seattle didn't shoot unless they were shot at first, and neither did the DEA. What was going on?

"Are you certain that they are cops? Cops don't do that. Could they have been from one of the Families?"

The initial success of the Asian gangs on the West Coast had brought them into serious competition with the old established Mafia criminal Families. There had been some bloodshed at first until a business arrangement could be worked out, but things had been peaceful lately. In addition to that, Deng had worked long and hard to get the peace treaty with the Chinese and Koreans so he could concentrate on moving the heroin, and this was an inopportune time for another turf battle.

Minh shook his head. "I don't think they're Mafia. Tuan said that after shooting our men, they stuck around and talked to the Seattle cops when they showed up."

"They've got to be some kind of Feds then."

"But what kind of Feds shoot first and talk later?" Minh sounded uneasy. "According to the old man at the shop, they didn't even give our men a chance. They just gunned them down. And no one has seen them around town before."

Deng had had his brushes with the DEA, but he had always been able to outsmart the Feds because they were required to operate within the law. And, for some reason he had never been able to understand, in the Land of the Free, the law always favored those who lived outside of it. Deng had heard vague rumors, however, about some shadowy federal agency that operated more like a B-grade-movie hit team than a law-enforcement agency. They shot first and never asked questions.

He wondered if his capturing Pham had anything to do with this. If it did, he had better find out about it before the situation got completely out of control. He didn't need any trouble with the Feds now. The heroin shipments were due to start coming in from Cam Ranh Bay next week, and nothing could be allowed to interrupt their distribution.

"Get Pham in here," Deng ordered. "I need to see what he knows about this."

Minh smiled. He would enjoy talking to his boyhood friend turned federal cop.

"OKAY," SCHWARZ SAID as he watched the last of the police cars drive off. "What's next on our agenda, Carl?"

"We check out the next place on our list."

"You want me to call 911 now?"

"Maybe we won't need them this time," Blancanales said.

"Fat chance of that."

Blancanales's hunch proved to be right. At their next stop, no one gave them any trouble at all. But then, they didn't learn anything there, either. No one had seen Pham, and no one knew anything about Deng.

"It's going to take a long time to find him doing it this way." Schwarz looked up at the leaden sky when they got back out on the street. It wasn't raining yet, but he could see it was coming.

"You got a better idea?" Lyons asked.

"Yeah."

"Give."

"Instead of running all over town asking every Viet we meet if he's seen Pham, why not go all the way to the top and ask Deng what happened to him?"

"Why not?"

A quick call back to the DEA task force gave them the address of Deng's headquarters. A drive-by revealed that it was a three-story brick structure that took up half a block of small shops. Around the side, a narrow alley ran the length of the block. The back side of Deng's building had only a single door, and it was in the middle of the windowless wall.

"This place's a fortress," Schwarz commented, peering up at the blank brick wall.

"It's a nice place for an illegal gambling den, though," Blancanales replied. "Quiet, not too many ways in. Pretty good setup."

"Not good enough, though," Lyons said. "There's also not too many ways out of the place, either. Pull over and let's take a closer look at it."

Schwarz parked the car on the far side of the alley opposite the door, and the three men got out. The alley was clear, so they opened the trunk of the vehicle, retrieved their bags and quickly changed into black fatigues, soft rubber-soled shoes and Kevlar body armor. Then they donned loaded combat harnesses, holsters and throat-mike radios.

Lyons retrieved his SPAS-12 and Colt Python, Schwarz his MP-5 and Blancanales his Uzi. Loading magazines and jacking rounds into the chambers, they flicked their weapons off safe as they approached the door.

While the others kept guard, Gadgets crouched and worked at the door lock with a pick.

"Get that thing open, damn it," Lyons growled, looking both ways down the alley. "We're exposed out here."

"Hold your water, Ironman. This thing isn't a nickel-and-dime lock. There." He turned the knob. "It's open."

"Wait!" He held up his hand when Lyons reached to go in. "There's an alarm."

"Fix it, quick!"

It took another few minutes and a small piece of wire for him to bypass the alarm. "Okay," Schwarz said as he opened the door, "now it's clear."

The hall inside was dark, and the three men hugged the wall for a few seconds while their eyes adjusted to the dim light. When they could see clearly, they spotted a door that provided entry to the first floor, and stairs leading up to the second floor at the end of the hall. Another locked door led to what apparently was a way down into the basement.

Lyons gestured for Schwarz to take the stairs going up. If this was the headquarters for Deng's operations, the man wouldn't have his office on the ground floor. The big boss would want to be up high where he wouldn't have to be bothered by the ash and trash wandering in and out.

The second-floor landing was empty. Lyons looked through the window in the door and saw apartments in the hall beyond. Obviously that wasn't what they were looking for, but there were no stairs leading from this landing up to the third floor. There had to be another stairwell, probably at the other end of the hall. He jerked his thumb toward the door, and Blancanales led off with Schwarz close behind him.

DENG PICKED UP the phone on the first ring. Minh's voice was tense. "We have armed men on the second floor."

"Are they police?"

"I can't tell. They're packing heavy firepower and wearing black SWAT-team uniforms. But they aren't marked, and they aren't wearing hats."

Deng thought fast. Anyone could wear SWAT-team black, but the Seattle PD always wore their police ID markings, and they always wore headgear. These men weren't regular cops, but they could be the people who had gunned down his two men that morning, which meant they were dangerous.

"How many men do you have here today?"

"Most of them are involved in the move, but there should be a dozen or so."

"Good. We should be able to take care of three men no matter who they are. Let them get up on the third floor and then take them out."

"No problem."

Deng reached into his desk drawer and took out a MAC-10 submachine gun. Slamming the magazine into the butt of the pistol grip, he pulled the bolt handle back to chamber a 9 mm round. There was no way that those guys could get past his men upstairs, but it didn't hurt to be ready just in case.

As Lyons had suspected, there was another stairwell at the end of the second-floor hall. Again, the landing was clear and they took up positions just inside the door. At the top of the stairs was an ornately carved red door that looked thick enough to be armored, as well as an electronic lock with a buzzer mounted on the wall. That meant that, more than likely, the landing was under electronic observation. He expected nothing less of a known criminal's headquarters.

Lyons pantomimed kicking open the door, and Blancanales nodded. Cautiously they approached the red door one step at a time. When they were in position, Lyons's fingers snapped out of his fist— one...two...three.

On the count of three, Blancanales hit the buzzer and when the lock clicked, planted his foot against the door and shoved it open. A barrage of fire greeted the opening door, but Able Team was hugging the wall in the hall outside. Schwarz had an M-26 fragmentation grenade in hand, the pin pulled, waiting. When the gunfire died down, he lobbed the lethal egg through the door. As soon as the explosion died away, the three men rushed through the open door.

Two bodies lay in the hallway, victims of Schwarz's grenade. Before they could clear the bodies, a third hardman stepped out from cover, the MAC-10 in his hands spitting flame.

Lyons staggered backward, his Kevlar body armor soaking up the 9 mm slugs. The assault shotgun in his hands roared in return, firing a full load of double-aught buckshot into the man's chest. The gunner flew backward in a spray of blood and collapsed against the wall.

Two more hardmen broke from cover, firing as they raced for an elevator at the far end of the room. Not stopping to take aim, Blancanales and Schwarz stitched them both from throat to crotch with long bursts of 9 mm bullets.

The first man was cut down in midstride, crumpling lifeless to the floor. The last gunner made it all the way to the elevator door before he died, his finger brushing against the call button. The double doors quietly slid back, and the interior lights came on as the elevator waited for its next passengers.

"It looks like an invitation to me." Schwarz eyed the open door.

"An invitation to get ourselves chopped," Blancanales growled.

"Let's get this over with." Lyons changed magazines as he headed for the elevator.

"Why not?" Schwarz shrugged. "I haven't gotten shot recently."

IN THE BASEMENT, six of Deng's men patiently waited for the arrival of the elevator from the top floor. Pushing the button for the sublevel had sounded an alarm, and they were ready for it. When the car reached the bottom and the outer doors retracted, they poured a fusillade of gunfire into the inner doors. Half a dozen submachine guns dumped their full magazines into the target.

The inner doors slowly opened, but revealed an empty elevator instead of the bleeding bodies the hardmen expected. One of Deng's men poked his head inside the car as if he didn't believe his eyes. Too late, he looked up to see the barrel of Lyons's shotgun in the open escape hatch in the ceiling. The guy took the full blast of 12-gauge buck in the face, dissolving his head into a bloody pulp.

Before his body hit the floor, a frag grenade arched out into the room and the other five scattered. Lyons hadn't pulled the pin on the grenade, but before the hardmen could take note of that fact, Able Team had dropped down out of hiding with weapons blazing. The five Vietnamese didn't last thirty seconds before they were taken permanently out of play.

The last shot had barely echoed away when a man stepped out of an office holding another man in front of him as a shield. Lyons recognized Pham and didn't have to ask to know that the guy holding the subgun to the DEA agent's head was the leader of the Black Fist, Tran Van Deng.

Dropping his SPAS, Lyons cleared leather with his Colt Python and snap-fired one shot. The .357 round took Deng right between the eyes, exploding out the back of his head.

Schwarz ran forward, reaching Pham's side before Deng's body hit the floor.

"I got Pham!" he called out. "Let's get out of here!"

"Where's out?" Blancanales asked, looking around the basement.

"Down this hall," Pham gasped.

CHAPTER FOURTEEN

"It was a pretty stupid thing for me to have done," Pham admitted as the paramedic in the DEA office treated his cuts and scrapes. "And I didn't even get much information out of it. All I really learned is that Deng was moving his headquarters to another location." He shook his head. "But I don't know where he was going."

"Why would he have been doing that?" Lyons wondered. "He had a perfect location there, particularly with that basement fortress."

Pham shrugged. "The obvious reason has to be that he was into something big, something that was bound to draw attention to him, and he wanted to drop out of sight. We've known for a long time where he was operating from, and anytime we had wanted to talk to him, we would have known exactly where to go. We didn't know anything about the basement hideout, that's true, but we would have discovered it soon enough. Obviously he knew that we were on to him and decided to set up shop someplace where we couldn't find him."

"You said that he appeared to be planning something else in addition to the move. You have any idea what that could have been?"

"Not really," Pham admitted. "But I did overhear that they were expecting something coming in soon from Cam Ranh Bay. From the way they were talking about it, it sounded important."

"Cam Ranh Bay is in Vietnam." Blancanales looked surprised. "I thought this was supposed to be a North Korean or Chinese operation."

"Maybe it's really a joint operation with all three nations involved," Schwarz said. "That would explain why the Vietnamese, Chinese and Korean gangs have quit shooting at one another here. Cooperation over there translates into peace on the streets here."

"There's got to be more to it than simply that." Lyons frowned. I can't see a terrorist organization dictating policy to American street gangs."

"I agree," Schwarz said, nodding, "but the Viets have got to be up to something. I can almost smell it."

"I'm also having a difficult time seeing a street-gang leader getting involved with a nuclear weapons hijacking," Blancanales said. "That's serious and could get a man in more trouble than he has years to work off. Gangs don't like to attract that kind of attention."

"Not unless there was something in it for him that we can't see," Schwarz interjected. "Gangs aren't into terrorism. It doesn't pay well enough. Gang scum do what they do for the money, not for a cause. They might use a nuke for extortion, yes, but not terrorism."

"But what if the terrorists who have the weapons need a gang to finance their operations for them?" Blancanales was thinking out loud. "Since the Russians went out of business and the Saudis wised up about supporting that crap, it's been difficult for them to get funding."

"But how could Deng's Black Fist gang have helped them?" Pham sounded skeptical. He knew drug operations, but terrorists were out of his league.

Blancanales shrugged. "The same way gangs finance themselves anywhere—they sell drugs, they run prostitutes or they pull off bank jobs."

"The drug connection could be a possibility," Pham said. "Vietnam has some of the best opium-growing conditions in the world. And with all the problems surrounding cocaine now, heroin is becoming the drug of choice again. We're getting more and more of it on the streets."

"But even so, that puts us back to the big question," Schwarz said. "What does heroin have to do with hijacked Russian nuclear warheads?"

"I don't have the slightest idea," Lyons admitted. "But I'd better let Barb know about this anyway. Maybe the Bear can make some kind of sense out of this."

AARON KURTZMAN WAS frustrated. With savage strokes of his powerful arms, he propelled his chair from one bank of computers to the next, as if he were in a wheelchair sprint race. As far as he was concerned, there was no problem that couldn't be solved if you gathered enough information about it and ran it through the data banks for analysis.

The problem this time was that he didn't have enough information yet to analyze. Even with the intelligence services of a dozen nations working day and night, not enough hard data was being developed. Since the successful conclusion of the Pusan operation, the reports had doubled. But most of it led nowhere. There had been no further sign of the missing warheads and no information to help him discover who was behind this.

However, even though he wanted more information, he could sense that the answer was already somewhere in his data banks. All he needed was time and it would all fall into place, but time was what they had the least of.

Nuclear warheads weren't plastique bombs in briefcases. If even one of them detonated, thousands of people could die—never mind the environmental impact. And there were nine more of them out there somewhere. . . .

"Aaron," Barbara Price said, "calm down. You've got to give this thing a little more time to develop. We simply don't have enough information yet. Finding that first bomb was a fluke. It's going to take time to find the rest of them."

"Tell that to Hal," he growled. "He's on my case big-time because the President is hounding him. If he'd leave me alone, I might be able to come up with something. I can handle pressure, but his calling all the time is driving me—"

The scrambled phone rang, and he snatched the handset from its cradle. "Kurtzman."

"Bear," Lyons said, "it's Ironman. I think we may have developed something here. I don't know what it has to do with our mission, but it's all we've been able to come up with so far."

"Give."

The Able Team leader quickly gave him a rundown on their activities for the day.

"You're at the DEA building?" Kurtzman asked.

"Right."

"Stay there. I'll get back to you."

"We'll be here," Lyons answered. "We're not too popular on the streets of Seattle at the moment."

As soon as Lyons hung up, Kurtzman was at his keyboard, punching in the codes to bring up the most recent data he had on drug-dealing operations and the Vietnamese. The information indicated that the Vietnamese government was working hard to have its country become the world's primary source of opium poppy production. There was even a tantalizing bit that indicated they had financed a modern lab to convert their raw opium into high-grade heroin.

There was nothing, however, to show that any of their activities were aimed at the United States. Everything showed that the Vietnamese had teamed up with the French criminal element to move their product, and it was all going to Europe.

If they had been working a drug interdiction mission, Lyons's information would have been interesting data. But it had little to do with tracking down stolen nuclear weapons. Or so it seemed right now. Lyons's idea that the Vietnamese were somehow financing terrorists through drug dealing sounded a little farfetched to him. Nonetheless, he stored the data in the personal computer of his brain as well as in his data banks.

He'd forward Lyons's report to Interpol and the French drug authorities. Maybe they could use the information.

GREGORI KLIMOV WAS also frustrated with the lack of progress. He knew, however, that he couldn't have done any better if he had been back in his own headquarters. In fact, he would have done far worse. Even in the glory days of the old KGB, the Russians had never had anything to match the intelligence-gathering capabilities of this facility.

And this was just the most covert tip of the American intelligence-gathering iceberg. When he thought of the capabilities of the CIA, the DIA and the military service intelligence arms combined with those of this place known as the Farm, it was no wonder that the old Soviet Union had never been able to keep up with the Americans in the covert operations arena. If Andropov and the other old hard-liners had had this kind of setup, they could have ruled the world like they had once dreamed of doing.

Even with their superiority, Klimov knew that the Americans would never try to dominate the world the way the Russians had planned to do. As he had seen, they plainly had the means to do it, but they didn't have the desire. And even if they had wanted to, they were all too often made impotent by their own ridiculous laws prohibiting the use of force in the foreign arena.

This current crisis was a good case in point. Even when the stolen warheads were found, political re-

straints would prevent the President from instantly
sending a military strike force against the terrorists.
Only after negotiations, political maneuvering and
empty threats would the President be able to act. By
then, it might be too late.

"WHAT DO YOUR PEOPLE have on recent Vietnamese drug-smuggling activities?" Price asked Klimov.

"Probably not as much as you have," the Russian admitted. "But we do know that they've
teamed up with the old French Connection people
and are funneling heroin into southern Europe. We
also think that they're working with the Iranians to
move the stuff into the Mediterranean through the
Kurds in Turkey."

"Have you heard anything about them trying to
move into the American market?"

"Our information is that they don't want to risk
trying it right now. They are still working very hard
to normalize relationships with your government so
they can get economic aid. They don't want to do
anything to jeopardize those negotiations."

Kurtzman nodded. "That fits in with what I have,
so I guess we have to keep on looking."

"AARON SAYS thanks a lot," Lyons told Schwarz
and Blancanales. "But he doesn't think much of our
idea that Cam Ranh Bay is the new drug export

center to support international terrorism. He says he can't find anything in his data bank to back it up."

"So what does Barb want us to do next?" Blancanales asked.

"We're getting tickets to L.A.," Lyons replied. "Barb wants us to poke around down there for a while, work the docks and talk to the DEA people again."

"So all of this was for nothing?"

"Not really," the Able Team leader said. "We got a few maggots off the streets and popped a bad-guy kingpin. That's not bad for a couple days work."

"What's the weather forecast down there?" Schwarz asked.

Lyons smiled. "They say a storm front's moving in, Gadgets, and they're expecting rain for most of the next three days."

Schwarz shrugged. "No big deal. At least it will be warm rain."

Lyons grinned. He hadn't mentioned the cold front moving in with the storm.

CHAPTER FIFTEEN

Pyongyang, North Korea

Major Lim Son Rae was not a happy man. He couldn't forget that the carefully planned delivery of the warhead to Pusan had been thwarted. His Vietnamese coconspirator, Thant, had counseled that he put their failure aside to concentrate on the next operation. But Lim couldn't get the failure out of his mind. He burned to know how and why his plan had failed. He wanted to find out who was responsible for this critical setback, and whoever they were, he wanted bloody revenge. No one could be allowed to interfere with his plans for the New Revolution.

The ninja assassin mission against the American businessmen in Pusan had also been his operation, and he had just learned that his team had been wiped out to the last man. Though he had no proof yet and the details were still coming in, he had a gut feeling that the two incidents were somehow linked. He would have to obtain more information from his agents before he would know for certain.

The Liaison Bureau's agent network in South Korea numbered in the hundreds. One of the fortunate things about the citizens of the decadent South was that since they had been so thoroughly corrupted by capitalistic greed, they would even betray their own fathers for money.

The thing that always amazed Lim, however, was how little money it usually took to turn the capitalists into willing agents of their own destruction. Particularly when he was dealing with the pampered students in the southern universities. Many times he didn't even need to pay them for their services. They willingly agreed to betray the government that fed, clothed and educated them, because they saw it as "oppressive."

When the New Revolution was successful and the two Koreas were one nation again, these same students would reap their reward for having helped bring the South's downfall. But it wouldn't be the reward they expected from the workers' paradise they had worked so hard for. Every last one of them would be taken out and executed for being traitors. Lim could have respect for an honorable enemy, but he had none at all for traitors. You could convert an enemy, but once a man had become a traitor, he would always be a traitor. If he had betrayed his country once, he would do it again and he could never be trusted again.

Until such time as he could give these people the reward they had earned, however, he would use this small army of traitors to his advantage. Lim reached for the phone on his desk. It was time to seek answers to questions.

SEVERAL HOURS LATER, Major Lim had some of the answers he wanted. One of the minor clerks in the Pusan police headquarters was a Liaison Bureau agent who had helped gather target information for the ninjas' mission for a small fee. The clerk's much younger wife longed for the trappings of the middle class, but the clerk's meager salary provided little room for extra comforts. The money he made from selling information to the North Koreans made his home life a little cheerier.

According to him, the men who were responsible for both eliminating the ninjas and discovering the warhead on the ship were a special team of commandos, sponsored by the Americans and brought in to deal with the ninja assassins. Unfortunately the clerk hadn't had access to the information about these men until after they had acted. Exactly who they were and whom they worked for, he didn't know yet, but he should before too long.

The fact that this mysterious team had been able to kill his ninjas meant that they were fighting men to be respected. But their finding the warhead before it was detonated had to have been luck. Every step of the operation had been carried out by his most trusted comrades, men whose devotion to the cause was beyond reproach. None of them could have possibly betrayed the mission, so the commandos' success had to have been pure, blind luck.

Though Lim had little respect for the Americans as a people, he knew the role that luck played in any operation and he prayed daily to the Goddess of Good Fortune. That this American-backed team had been able to eliminate his ninjas as well as capture the warhead only meant that the goddess had smiled on *them*. To counter this, Lim knew that he would have to bring the goddess even greater gifts so she would turn her face to him again. The gift she cherished most was a well-laid plan. The Goddess of Good Fortune smiled on those who did everything in their power to create their own good fortune themselves.

The next thing he needed to know was exactly where these six men were staying in the South. If they were still in Pusan, that was so much the better.

While he didn't have another ninja team in the South to send against these new enemies, he still had an extensive network of deep-cover agents he could use. Most of these were people who had stayed behind in the South at the end of the Korean War. They had integrated themselves into the southern society, and some had even reached positions of responsibility in the police and government. They had patiently waited for years to be called upon to do something for their cause, and the time had finally come.

None of them were aware of Lim's plans for the New Revolution, but it wasn't necessary that they know anything about that. It was only necessary that they follow their orders, and Lim had no doubt in his mind that they would do that. Following orders without question was the bedrock of communism, and they were all good Communists.

Whoever these meddlers were, lucky or not, they were as good as dead.

Picking up his phone, Lim called a local soup shop. By ordering extra peppers with his noodle soup, he set up a meeting with one of his New Revolution cell members. By tonight, the deep-cover agents in the South would have their activation orders.

He would locate these commandos and he would have his vengeance.

THE HARDEST PART of any mission for Bolan and Phoenix Force was the waiting. Even with almost every intelligence service of the free world feeding a steady stream of information into Aaron Kurtzman's computer bank, Stony Man still didn't have a lead on the rest of the warheads. Once they were located it would be a relatively simple matter to go in after them. No matter where they were being held, one way or the other, they could be neutralized or eliminated. But before that could happen, they had to be found. Until they were, the Stony Man warriors would have to wait for a break.

Part of the problem with fighting terrorists was discovering their base of operations. Sometimes knowing their demands on what they were after provided a key. But so far, no one had any idea what they were trying to accomplish. Had this been the Middle East, the warrior would have known what their aims were—the embarrassment of the United States or the destruction of Israel. But there was no identifiable goal this time.

Barbara Price had briefed him on the Russian liaison officer's theory about the tie-in with the hardline Communist elements in China and North Korea, who wanted to overthrow the current regimes. It seemed fairly well thought out to him, and it fitted in with several other intelligence summaries he had read recently about the political situation in the Asian Communist states.

Unlike Kurtzman, Bolan could look at Klimov's theory without linking it to the man who had come up with it. He didn't like the idea of having to work the Russian any more than the Bear did. But the man was a Far East expert, and it could very well be that he knew what he was talking about.

If his theory was correct, however, it presented several major obstacles that wouldn't be easy to overcome. The biggest problem was that it would be difficult to get a handle on these particular hard-liners. Since they were in opposition to their current governments, they would already be in deep cover, hiding from their own internal security forces. Even if they could be identified and located, moving against them would involve the risk of going to war with Red China or North Korea.

Speculation about that was futile right now, though. There would be time enough to worry about that when the weapons were found. Until then, he would check in with the Farm every two hours while the other men caught up on their sleep.

GARY MANNING WAS RESTING in his BOQ room when he heard a knock on the door.

"Come in."

The knock came again.

"Okay, okay, I'm coming."

He opened the door and saw a middle-aged Korean woman standing next to a wheeled cart loaded with paper towels, toilet-paper rolls and cleaning materials. "I clean you room?" she asked.

"It's okay. I don't need anything."

"So sorry," she insisted, bowing her head. "I have to clean room today."

Manning shrugged. "Go ahead, lady," he said as he stepped aside to let her in. Who was he to stand in the way of someone who had a job to do?

The cleaning woman went into the bathroom first, and he heard the sounds of water pouring into the sink. To get out of her way, he went over to the second-story window that overlooked the runway. As he watched a plane take off, he heard a slight scuffling noise behind him.

Only well-trained, lightning-fast reflexes saved him as a piano-wire garrote started down over his head. He got his left hand inside the loop. The wire caught on his watchband, but still bit into his neck and wrist. He tried to twist around, but she had her knee in his back, forcing him to the floor.

Korean Intelligence liaison officer Kim Tae Ro was walking down the hall of the BOQ when he noticed that the door to Gary Manning's room was partially open. Since he needed to talk to the Canadian demolition man anyway, he stopped and stood on the threshold.

"Mr. Christie," he called out. "It's Kim, do you have a minute?"

He heard a scuffling noise inside the room and a crash as something hit the floor.

Kim kicked the door, slamming it against the inside wall. He saw the big Canadian on his knees, his hands up to his neck. Standing behind him was someone who looked like one of the BOQ's cleaning women.

The woman turned, dropped into a fighting stance and rushed him.

Dropping into a fighting stance himself, Kim's foot snaked out toward the woman's left knee. She pivoted out of the way and let fly with a kick of her own. Kim caught the woman's booted foot with both hands and shoved backward. She crashed against the wall, but rebounded strongly.

Whoever she was, she was good, but no match for Kim. Feinting to the left, he planted his left foot and swung his right in a high kick. The blow connected, and Kim felt the cartilage in the woman's neck give way. There was a difference in being well trained in a martial art and killing a person with it.

The woman crumpled to the floor, her face contorted and turning purple as she clawed at her crushed throat. A few seconds later, her eyes rolled back in their sockets, her feet drummed against the floor, her back arched and she was dead.

Kim knelt beside her, his fingers pressed against her carotid to confirm that she was dead.

"You okay?" he asked Manning, as he held out his hand to help him up.

The Canadian grasped Kim's forearm and got to his feet, the garrote in his hands. "Thanks, I'm fine now."

He shook his head. "Damn! She almost had me there."

"What happened?"

"I let her come in to clean the room and made the mistake of turning my back on her. The next thing I knew, she was going for me with this garrote. I got one hand inside the loop and it caught on my watchband, which is the only thing that saved me."

He rubbed the wire cut on his wrist. "I'd better get a bandage on this."

"Your neck's been cut, too," Kim said. "Let's get you to the base hospital and have those wounds seen to."

Manning put his hand to the right side of his neck and felt the blood. "Hell, I didn't even feel it cut me!"

"Piano wire will kill you before you even know that your throat's been cut."

"I need to warn the rest of the guys."

"We'll call them from the hospital." Kim took his arm and led him toward the door. "Clamp your hand over the neck wound before you bleed to death."

CHAPTER SIXTEEN

On the first floor of the BOQ, three of the other Phoenix Force warriors had also had visitors. James, McCarter and Encizo had answered knocks on their doors to confront men posing as air-conditioner repairmen and telephone technicians. However, unlike Manning, they hadn't taken their eyes off their unexpected visitors for a second.

McCarter's repairman claimed that he had to check the telephone and was led over to the night-stand by the bed. When the man fumbled trying to take the bottom of the phone apart, McCarter backed away from him and quietly drew his pistol from the holster hanging in the closet. When the Korean rose with a throwing dagger in his hand, McCarter calmly put a bullet in the guy's head.

James's assassin had chosen to attack him the instant he stepped into the room. Though somewhat taken by surprise, the Phoenix Force commando instantly recovered and in the process took out his opponent permanently.

Encizo watched his man walk to the phone by his bed, his eyes taking in everything in the room. When the Korean knelt and opened his toolbox, the Cuban saw him reach for the hilt of the fighting knife lying in the top tray. Not waiting to see what was going to happen next, Encizo delivered a kick to the back of his neck, snapping the man's spine.

Bolan and Katz, however, hadn't been in their rooms. They were in the base in a radio conference with Aaron Kurtzman and Barbara Price back in Virginia. It had been several days since the American government had been informed of the loss of the Russian warheads, and the situation in Washington and Moscow was becoming even more tense.

At Kurtzman's request, Bolan was going over in detail yet again the recovery of the warhead from the North Korean ship, in case he had left something out.

An Air Police captain entered the communications room and rushed up to Bolan. "Colonel Pollock?"

"Yes."

"There's been a problem with your men at the BOQ, sir."

"What happened?"

"They were attacked by infiltrators."

"Was anyone hurt?"

"One man received a cut on his neck, but none of the others were injured, sir."

Bolan didn't bother to ask about the health of the infiltrators; he already knew. "Where are they?"

"They're at the base hospital, with the injured man. I have transportation outside, sir. I'll take you to them."

"Let's go."

WHEN BOLAN and Katz arrived at the base hospital, Gary Manning was having a long cut across the side of his neck stitched closed. He already had a bandage taped around his left wrist. The other three Phoenix Force warriors were armed and watching the door and windows.

"What happened, Gary?" Bolan asked.

"I guess someone doesn't like us being here." Manning shook his head. "They sent a cleaning lady to tell me that we've overstayed our welcome."

"A woman?"

"Yeah, a cleaning woman who had a piano wire garrote tucked in with her window cleaner and paper towels." He shook his head. "I'd have been in a world of hurt if Kim hadn't been coming down the hall and saw that my door was open. He crashed the party and peeled her off of my back."

He winced when the medic made another stitch. "You should see that Kim guy in action. I think he could even teach you a thing or two."

"There," the medic said, snipping the last suture. "That should do it. Just make sure that you don't put any strain on those stitches for the next week or so."

Manning slowly moved his head from side to side. "Right."

Seeing Kim walk into the treatment room, Bolan went to meet him.

"How is he?" the Korean asked.

"I understand that thanks to you, he's fine. There was no serious damage."

"I am just glad that I was there at the right time. I was coming to tell you that there had been no more information from the ship's captain. We now believe that he knew nothing of the warhead. But when I passed Mr. Christie's door, I remembered that I needed to ask him a question about the bomb-disposal procedure. When he didn't answer my call, I heard a noise and kicked the door open."

"It doesn't matter why you were there. I want to thank you."

"No thanks are necessary."

Katzenelenbogen changed the subject. "Do you have anything on the attackers yet?"

Kim shook his head. "According to my headquarters, they are all completely clean. None of them have any association with known enemy agents, either North Korean or Chinese. Until now, they have all been model citizens."

"They're somebody's deep-cover agents then."

"We agree," Kim said. "But whose agents, and why were they sent to kill you?"

"Obviously," Bolan replied, "we're getting in the way of somebody's plans."

"But what plans? We have still not had any demands or anyone claiming responsibility for the incident."

"Considering what we found on the ship, I'd say that whoever was responsible for putting that warhead on board is planning to turn the entire Pacific basin into a nuclear wasteland. I think that this is more than just another North Korean attack against the South."

"We still don't know, though," Katz interjected, "what they think they are trying to do. This is not following the usual terrorist attack pattern. As you pointed out, Kim, we haven't had any demands, there's no list of prisoners to be released, no ransom money to be paid, nothing. Whoever these people are, we don't have the slightest idea why they are doing this."

"That's what Aaron is supposed to be telling us," Bolan pointed out.

"He'd better start telling us something soon. I don't like flying blind, and I don't like being a target. This should have been a secure area for us. The base commander is going to have to answer some questions about how those people got in here."

"I can answer that myself," Kim stated. "All of them had valid local work-force passes. The BOQ is not a security area, so the workers come in on local hire passes. If their face matches their pass, they get in the gate."

"We're going to have to see that something is done about that."

"It's already been done," Kim replied. "Along with an increased Air Police alert at the gates, we have put male and female Korean agents there to search and question all of the local workers."

"That's a good start." Katz patted his shoulder holster. "But we'll be doing a few things on our own, as well."

"WE'VE SURE AS HELL rattled someone's cage," Aaron Kurtzman said as he scrolled down the list of the enemy dead in the attack at the BOQ. "That was a suicide mission. Even if they had been able to take out our people, they would never have gotten off the base. The questions are, what did we do to get that kind of response and whose cage was it?"

"From the identities of the attackers—" Barbara Price read the screen over his broad shoulders "—it looks like at least half of them were Chinese deep-cover agents activated for that single mission. Apparently our man Klimov was right all along. The Chinese and the North Koreans are involved in this thing together.''

"Do you want me to arrange to have the team moved to a more secure location?''

Price thought for a moment. "No, I think we should leave them where they are. Now that they know they've been targeted, Mack and Katz won't be caught off guard again. If we move them, the enemy will have to waste time finding them and I don't want that to happen." She smiled briefly. "I'm kind of hoping that they'll send someone else against our guys so they can get us a prisoner this time.''

It wasn't surprising that none of the would-be assassins had survived their contact with Phoenix Force. Few people did. But the way this operation was going, the Farm desperately needed them to capture one of the enemy for interrogation. If they could get the right man for a few hours, they could solve this crisis once and for all.

"Mack isn't going to like being a stationary target," Kurtzman commented.

"He's been a target before," she replied. "He knows the drill.''

MACK BOLAN WHOLEHEARTEDLY agreed with Price's decision to leave them where they were instead of sending them into hiding. Now that they had personally been targeted, he knew the risk of keeping too high a profile. But, at the same time, he knew that Stony Man desperately needed interrogation subjects. Had even one of the attackers survived, they could be well on their way to obtaining a viable lead.

But they hadn't survived. Casualties were always high when Phoenix Force found itself in a combat situation. More so in close-quarters hand-to-hand fighting. The assassins had gone to the BOQ to take out the Stony Man warriors. Like many before them, they'd come up short. Still, had it not been for Kim's timely assistance, it might not have gone as well as it had. The Korean Intelligence agent proved to be a good man to have around in the crunch.

Bolan decided that Hal Brognola should be made aware of Kim's assistance. A presidential citation was out of the question, but perhaps a word of praise from the man's own government on the behalf of America would let Kim know that his timely assistance had been appreciated.

Of all the men in the world, Bolan knew how lonely it could get for a man in the counterterrorist business. It seemed that for every threat that was eliminated, three more sprang up in its place. It was a war without end, and a war where all too often the heroes went to their graves without recognition for their efforts. At least Kim would know that someone had noticed his efforts.

MAJOR LIM SON RAE wasn't pleased when he got the report of the failure of the attack on the Americans at Pusan Air Force Base. Whoever these Americans were, they were either very good or they were very lucky. But since the report had indicated that none of his agents had survived the assassination attempt, he had to think that it had been more skill than luck. The fact that they had been able to take out the entire ninja unit in Pusan should have told him something about their capabilities. And that was what puzzled him.

His ninjas were among the best-trained warriors in the world. Man for man, they could hold their own against any of the world's special forces units. So, how had they been defeated? His agent had positively identified the victors as Americans, but they were no Americans Lim could identify. They were too good. He had, however, heard rumors of a shadowy American-backed clandestine-operations group that specialized in counterterrorist operations. Wherever they showed up, death followed.